To Yolanda,
Thank you so much for helping my mother and I with everything -

POLYVERSE
PART I:
THE FULCRUM

PHILIP H. ISLES

2000

ISBN 0-7414-0509-1

Published by:

Buy Books on the web.com
519 West Lancaster Avenue
Haverford, PA 19041-1413
Info@buybooksontheweb.com
www.buybooksontheweb.com
Toll-free (877) BUY BOOK
Local Phone (610) 520-2500
Fax (610) 519-0261

Buy Books on the web.com

Printed in the United States of America

Printed on Recycled Paper

Published September-2000

For Margaret and Barbara, Monet of mothers,
And Ben, the amnesiac Buddha

IMPORTANT!
THIS IS NOT A NORMAL BOOK. IT DOES NOT START ON PAGE 1. TURN TO CHAPTER 0, THEN FOLLOW THE INSTRUCTIONS ACCORDING TO YOUR DECISIONS

This book has been designed to bring you, the reader, into the story. My first experiment with 'interactive fiction.' Each decision is designed to help readers investigate their indiviual orientation according to love and fear. As the story unwinds in a way unique to each reader, it becomes a customized tool for increasing one's awareness of these fundamental opposites of our universe. By observing the consequences of these choices, it is my hope that the reader will attain a higher awareness of love and the realization that it is, ultimately, always the right decision.

Acknowledgements

This book was written through me, from that which we collectively know as 'love.' I am no more than a fusion of the elements below.

My brothers Nick, the stubborn Ronin, and Adam, the placid lawman.

The Jeromes: Hotel California of the East. Ginger ale. The screen porch. Camilla the fish. Cinderella's daughter—Ash. Paula, secret harbinger of rightness. Brian, cyclops with a hidden heart. But most importantly, Shane, whose innocent simplicity has taught me more than any complicated thing.

The Weisman family: My reference for all virtues. Lorenzo, the father all fathers ascribe to. Stanley, proof that youth does not decay. Alexia 'Pegs,' my first encounter with the remarkably awesome results that middle-child syndrome can bring. Melissa, the ideal summit to which these youths aspired. But most importantly, Thomas, the quintessential friend, partner in my fundamental humor and the one who made me see how useful the consideration of a consequence can be.

William Winkler, who taught me the importance of so many miscellaneous things.

Francesco, who showed me the weapon that some call irony, but we both know as the ultimate definer for the world we share.

Matteo, the coke addict.

Lincoln and Melina, two notions of confusing opposites.

My greatest teachers: 'Baz', Bill Zavatsky, Mr. McCahill, Mr. King, Mr. Burbank, and Mr. Moore.

My mother, the coerced critic.

Philip, perpetual bachelor.

CONTENTS

Chapter 29

Rain had married someone five years ago and was walking with their two-year old son through the concrete city's brutal heat, whose tarred black streets and sidewalks of cement had been baking in the sun all day. It had been a long afternoon at the fair with her kid, who was not saying anything because, in a plastic zip-lock bag of water he was holding swam a goldfish he had won from a game-booth. Rain did not expect the fish to live for very long, but she was glad to have it with them as they walked towards their home. Without it, he would have whined the whole way back.

They could have been in Little Italy or Chinatown. Chicago or Detroit. No, definitely not Detroit—but the point is that it does not matter where they were, only that the heat was fierce and all that kept her toddler from a tantrum was his newfound friend, the goldfish, whom he had decided to call Camilla.

Hoping to escape the heat, they had gone inside a Ben and Jerry's. But then Rain saw a fat man, and left.

She passed several bars on the way home and then, no longer able to tolerate the temperature, turned around and went back into the nearest one. They were both so sweaty that her son's hands slipped out of her grasp when she stopped. Reluctantly, he looked away from the fish to see what she was doing.

A gin and tonic came to mind and so she stepped inside. The place was empty when she entered, but as soon as she sat down with the boy a sound of rushing water stopped and a bartender came out of the back. She was expecting him to say something about the minor sitting next to her. That he was looking at him with an unreadable expression made her feel even more frustrated than she had felt outside. But all he did was ask her what she wanted.

Sammy Aldo, a man who didn't give a damn, entered the bar and sat down at a table in the corner. He was dressed in a white suit, causing him to stand out from the dark interior of the bar. He asked the man behind the bar for a tall glass of water with no ice. He watched Rain for momentarily and then lost interest.

Everyone was hot. Rain savored the taste of her drink while the bar tender washed his hands. Her son was focused on the fish and Sammy wrapped his hands around the glass. Rain had finished half her drink and was finally beginning to relax when suddenly the zip-lock bag split open and the fish fell on the floor. Instantly, the boy began to cry. The bar-tender was gone again and when she looked around the only person there was Sammy Aldo. The man who didn't give a damn.

And Sammy Aldo raised the water to his lips and finished off the water in a slow, continuous gulp. No longer able to tolerate the screaming, Sammy extinguished his cigarette and left.

The boy's shouts had already started to reverberate inside her skull. Soon enough the fish had ceased its desperate quivering and all that could be heard was the boy. It was going to be an even longer day. Rain wondered if her lack of sympathy today would resurface in the boy's therapy one day, when he was much older.

Go to Part II

Chapter 5

Once, when we were much younger, Alexander called me on the last night of Christmas vacation. On his way back from France, he had found an empty book of matches on his seat. Having been bored, he turned the matches over in his hands to find that a day and month had been written in pencil onto the back.

He had thought it was a sign of some kind. An omen. I do not remember what the exact date had been, but I do remember that the date came and went with no events of any significance and both of us had forgotten by the year after.

I like to imagine—or even assume—that the date on those matches was the same date we flew back to America almost sixty years later. There is no reason why the dates should match, but then, there is no reason why they shouldn't. Alexander was so convinced that something important would happen to him on that date that ever since he told me about the matchbook, I thought about it each time something important happened in his life. The day he met his wife and the day he married her. Each day he found out she was pregnant and each day his children had been born. The seemingly infinite number of days and nights in which he called me with some momentous thought that he could not bare to hold alone.

All of these dates could have been the one on the matchbook, so is it not best that we both forgot the actual date? For each uncanny coincidence that fuels our curiosity about the universe, there are an infinite number of others that pass unnoticed. We are fortunate to be unaware of them in the same way an audience is fortunate not knowing a magician's secret. If we were aware of all the secrets held within the universe, would we not feel jaded?

Alexander chain-smoked Merit ultra-lights. Smoking is prohibited in airports. He didn't believe in prescription drugs, yet took tranquilizers when he flew. He blamed his dislike of flying on an experience he once had in Guatemala as a child. The airport had accidentally exploded. Glass windows had come down in sharp, solid clouds of rain and thrown his family in different directions. Everyone came out alive. None returned to Guatemala.

This being said, you can imagine how happy he was to be flying across the Atlantic Ocean with me. Although we had first class seats, he looked as though we were stowaways, about to be caught at any second in some thievery of distance. I had given up trying to calm him down. However, I continued my attempts at making him laugh, for humor had been the basis of our life-long friendship. Although my body had grown old and ached in many different places, all pain vanished when I laughed.

We had been traveling through Europe with Hermes once, just after graduating high school, stuck in a train somewhere in Spain—the southern-most part of Spain—in the middle of July. We were in a metal car, beneath the mid-day sun, unable to wait outside because we did not know when it would start moving again. The seats had ceased to feel like leather or even the imitation leather that they were actually made of. It felt more like a second layer of skin that we had shed long ago, but was still instinctively trying to re-bind itself with our damp, sweaty bodies. A lady had walked in with an open cardboard box, rambling in Spanish with a singsong voice. Everyone in the train was looking at her, and Alexander—being the only one who knew the language—informed Hermes and I that she was singing to a young bird in the box that she was carrying under her arm. She was telling the bird in the nicest possible way that it was probably about to die from heat exhaustion. The insanity in this—while enough to disturb me in hindsight—caused the three of us to laugh so recklessly that my stomach hurt the following day. Between the three of us, there had been enough laughter to conduct several miracles; one of them being an escape from the unbearable hit within the motionless oven.

So I tried to distract him as we flew Westwards. For the most part, it was useless. He kept his eye on the computerized map that his miniature television screen displayed, watching the small plane icon drag a thin red line from East to West at an agonizingly slow pace. It made me wonder how stupid the airlines must be to offer a visual clock on the same monitors that were meant to take our minds off the time.

When we had been seniors in high school and were in the process of completing our college essays, I remember encouraging him to submit an experience he had had once while returning from a fencing tournament. He had been bumped up to first class, and after charming a stewardess into mixing cocktails for him, noticed the person next to him at the window. He had described him to me as tall, dressed in black, and resembling Santana. He wore sunglasses and swung a necklace back and forth on his right index finger, a golden crucifix attached to the end.

This man had asked Alexander what he wanted to study in school, and after hearing that he had not yet decided between art or science, asked what the difference was between the two. Alexander had walked off the plane a different person, and I like to think that Harvard recognized the significance in such an event upon reading his essay. If so, one more moment of significance in Alexander's life occurred while doing that which he feared most.

I would look away from the window on my right at different times throughout the flight to see how he was doing. When his eyes were closed, I wondered what he was thinking, for what does one think when trying to ignore his thoughts? He answered my questions as curtly as possible, as if being interrogated, or as a father might answer his six-year-old son while trying to fix a flat tire.

It was no use, and I eventually gave up somewhere over the Atlantic Ocean, turning to the stars outside my window or movies on the television. Or my dreams. Sometimes even the map to check on the thin red line.

It seemed that both of us had only just attained some kind of slumber when we were woken by the captain on the intercom. The plane was shaking harder than I thought a plane was capable of shaking without breaking, causing my vision of Alexander to become distorted. I did not know what the pilot was saying, because the noise of the shaking plane was too loud. However, no one was seriously panicking until the oxygen masks dropped down and we all realized that the situation was serious.

I expected Alexander's eyes to be closed for some reason, but when I looked to see if he had managed to attach the mask onto his face, they were wide open. He had fixed them on some unseen point of reference between the top of the seat in front of him and the ceiling of the plane. The mask was already strapped around his face before others had only just noticed them. However, I did not think it would help him that much, because he had clamped his teeth so tightly that his lips were stretched back to his molars and I could see the profile of his teeth outside the confines of the plastic yellow cup.

The plane was going to crash, and we were crashing with it.

The thought that I might be unable to exchange a final word with my dear friend before we died caused a fierce frustration that erased all other feelings. That I was dying did not matter—only dying before saying all the things I should have said. Instead of prayer or screams of panic, all I felt was disappointment. Perhaps this explains the speed at which my consciousness was flowing as our plane approached the ground.

I am almost dead, I thought, *We are falling so quickly—several hundred tons of potential energy that gravity has finally realized. How ironic is the fact that a force of attraction is the thing that will ultimately kill me? Is that why broken hearts can hurt so much once they have fallen in love?*

I was laughing helplessly, oblivious to the panic around me. I laughed so hard I doubled over and the other passengers around me must have thought that I was following emergency procedures.

But Alexander had known me long enough to differentiate the sources of my tears. He knew that I was having some ironic thought. He knew I was not going crazy or considering the crash ahead of us. A fire had started somewhere in the back, the screams were getting louder. The stewardesses had disappeared and I wondered whether they got parachutes or not. Neatly dressed women, sinking from the sky onto some city street or picnic table was making me laugh louder. As if some guy who is just a normal, lonely guy might pray one day in the name of his lonely heart and the stewardess who served my ginger ale fell into his convertible from the clouds above him. They drive into the sunset, but ever so slowly, due to some traffic delay that is caused by a plane that crashed on its way to Kennedy.

The plane was getting closer to the ground and I was laughing harder. Alexander was looking at me from behind the big yellow cup and I thought he resembled a clown with some kind of awful disease in his nose. The normal red nose of a clown had mutated into some terrible tumor that required a nasal colostomy bag to drain viral fluids to keep it from exploding.

I could not help myself from thinking these strange things and wanted desperately to tell my friend what I was thinking. His eyebrows were all scrunched up in confusion, and I felt encouraged to attempt some kind of explanation. I pointed to my oxygen mask and made a funny face.

Alexander starts to laugh with me: Go to chapter 8
Alexander does not laugh at all: Go to chapter 29

Chapter 8

Many might have been surprised to see Alexander and myself in such hysterics as we made our way towards the ground. But if you have ever had a friendship based on humor you would understand completely. The closer we got to the ground, the more we made faces at each other, with references to cancerous clowns and horses that had accidentally gotten stuck in their bags of oats.

I had never been inside a fire before. I was surprised that it did not feel hot. Then I remembered how bad the heat had been inside that train in Spain and knew why nothing hurt.

We did not know about the storm that was causing our plane to crash. If we had survived, and had been able to watch the news surrounding the weather that night, we would have learned that it had come from nowhere. It crashed our plane before the weather teams had picked a name for it. Because of this, the media dubbed it Jane Doe. Years later, a graduate student studying meteorology did his dissertation on Jane Doe, and concluded that it had either originated in the Bermuda Triangle or was caused by shifting tectonic plates beneath the upper east side of Manhattan island.

There had never been a storm that caused two bolts of lightning to strike the same place on the ground, and yet this storm was doing it repeatedly, ruthlessly striking down various objects on the same open field our plane was about to crash in. At precisely the same moment we hit the ground and in exactly the same place, two enormous tentacles of radiant electricity connected the storm to the ground and the tip of our plane, forming an upside down pyramid with Alexander and myself at the very tip.[1]

Because of our laughter and because the force of nature's electricity and because the power of a pyramid in certain places can do many a mysterious thing, our minds and souls

[1] See Illustration 2

were absent when our bodies hit the ground. With a force unknown by time and space, we felt ourselves pulled back through the cosmos, returning through the courses of our lives and even farther back, before we were born. We were watching the history that lead up to our own existence, passing our places of conception and beyond the thoughts that made us had even come about within our parents' minds.

We spun around and around each other, in the form of a double helix, revolving back and forth between each other's pasts, until we were thrown into two other lives, and were watching ourselves grow up from babies into gentlemen. These gentlemen became best friends, and when the journey that had started in the laughter prior to our deaths was over, we were seated in a large, antiquated library, looking at each other in our newfound bodies, totally in awe of our experience.[2]

Even stranger though, was the people we had incarnated. I was looking at my father Kyo as a young man. We did not need to say each other's name to know who we had become. Alexander was now in my father's body, and I, undoubtedly, was in the body of Ashta, the man who would one day become Alexander's father.

We had been playing a game of chess beside a fire in a large, empty library. Neither of us could remember the subject of our conversation though, for we had just had the same experience, and were trying to absorb the fact that we had turned into our fathers, and were presumably sitting in the land from which they came.

Go on to part II

---

[2] See Illustration 3

Chapter 64

I walked with Hermes towards Antonia's party. He had that look in his eyes—the one that made me feel at peace, as if assuring me that all my aspirations had a chance of being realized. Related by reality, we felt good within each other's presence. We walked in stride together, talking of the time we had spent apart. Everyone was walking towards the party. While the main crowd was up front, we dragged behind with a pace of our own—we would get there when we were ready. Neither of us wanted to see what we had already seen too much of. Nevertheless, we withheld a premature departure, hoping that we might find something interesting. I had left the lovers on the couch and taken it upon myself to dig deeper through the magazines and mobile phones, to see if anything lied beneath.

The group walked in rhythm, directed by the unique scent that every New York preppy high school house party smells of; beepers and phones ringing like a futuristic herd of cattle. Rather than tumbleweed or dust, Hermes and I rode in a wake of cigarette smoke and designer perfume. Elders walking dogs along the street stepped cautiously onto the other side.

Antonia's house was an immaculate five-story brownstone between First and Second Avenue. The top two floors held the party, meaning that one had to pass through the first three uncontaminated floors of her voice, which included her parents. That was the part I hated most about those parties; parents and doormen who knew what was going on, but did not have the power or the courage to intervene.

Tasteless smoke and the smell of soapy beer pervaded through the stories of the house in melancholy waves of gaseous clouds. It was hard to breathe, hard to see. Some kids danced in the corners, others did drugs in other corners, couples kissed passionately in even more corners. One would never think the music could be capable of such an influence, but it managed to effect the partygoers on a deeper level of the psyche. Although the music was loud, the kids seemed to be in touch with the energies of the party itself, not just the sounds from the stereo. The music only illustrated this distinctive pulsing, as did the clouds of smoke and fleeting moments of eye contact. Reverberations you could feel, become controlled by, lose judgement in. No one wanted to care, they wanted relief from a week of school and responsibility—to be wild before returning to the level on which society operates. I am not going to describe the party for you word for word, or tell you everything I saw. I know that you yourself will see them, or see them in your dreams sometimes, occasionally thinking of them in the same way Polaroids depress you, even if they stand as records of great times.

We ascended her round staircase as if taking turns on some carnival ride of sinister control, spiraling upwards towards the highest floor. I used the banister knobs to anchor my weight as I spun around to each consecutive floor. Her stairs were lined with plush carpeting, stained with ashes of cigarettes that her fellowship of guests had casually tossed away. People were lined up against the walls as we approached the party's nucleus—Antonia's bedroom. What more could they ask for? These children sitting on the pathway to her room held no desire for independence. They wanted to be receptors—to receive commands and do as they were told. I had the sense of rushing towards a vital organ in a body full of cells.

We entered Antonia's room, where a velvet red couch had been placed in the center. One of those fifties against the eighteenth century jobs that radiate a certain coolness because of their new age design. Three girls sat on it with tight turtlenecks and scarves that flowed around their necks. Taut pants that clung to hips and thighs . . . long hair to illustrate the rapid spinning of their heads. Perfect, desirable bodies, envied by both sexes. Their make-up glistened on the surface of their faces, as if to magnify their trademark smiles. Their eyes reflected light from two cheap lamps in corners of the room.

It appeared that what they wanted most was someone to decide for them as well, rather than direct the line of kids—or even themselves—that I had passed to get there, taking orders from the glossy pages on their laps. They were fighting over a magazine. I can't remember the name, but I recall the picture of some skinny blonde in front. They debated. They shouted with frustration when the magazine was taken from them. I could not help myself from watching.

"Let me see the article! It's my turn!"
"No! It's mine! You had it last, I want to look!"
"Oh shut up, both of you were wrong, it's MY turn!"

We escaped, moving onwards to a den upstairs, feeling a sense of desperation after watching the bondage below. I went ahead of Hermes to a separate room, holding our bottle of Smirnoff as catalyst for our departure. Hermes was flirting with a girl he did not wish to talk to while I sat in some room, surrounded by mirrors and images that traced Antonia's lifetime through rows of family photographs.

We closed the door and Hermes hit the phone with the same passion that I felt consumed by. We wanted to leave, desperately returning pages from his beeper and trying to recall our other options. We felt surrounded by that everlasting line of nameless children, who were talking a language I did not want to understand. Although I had no urge to look at my reflection, there were too many mirrors and I could not ignore my own image. I was not surprised to see myself in a tired, sorry looking state. I wanted desperately to talk to that image, but knew it wouldn't be of any use. No matter how hard I might try to reach the other side, everything would keep on going in the same old way. The mirror would continue to obey.

Hermes got up and we walked about the room in preparation for departure. Apparently, Hermes had found a better place. There were two folding doors that, placed together, had blocked us from the party. We each grasped a door and allowed the cloud of fumes and alcohol to find us once again, returning us inside the festival of desperation that had spread like cancer through the hallways of Antonia's house. We tried to ease our way downstairs with as little eye contact as was necessary, apologetic speeches in our head for whoever might attempt to trap us there. We knew how much those parties were like quicksand, where all one wants to do is leave. You may love the sand—on beaches, with margaritas and tans, but when mixed within the pits of carnal desires, filled to the top of the glass with anxious acts of envy, it becomes more than just a pitfall. It fools you into thinking that it is your friend, then harms your real friends—dragging them in as well with the trust you took so long to build.

We had almost made it out when Olivia fell into Hermes and me, supporting herself with our shoulders, balancing her head towards us so her eyes—which made me think of Oriental butterflies—connected with the both of us. On our pilgrimage towards the party we had passed Olivia, emaciated by bad wisdom and distorted mirrors, vomiting the lining of her stomach between a black Honda and a white Ford. I remembered the white turtleneck and gray flannel skirt all the girls had been made to wear when we went to grammar school together. Her friends were holding the long black hair behind her head, away from the stream of bile that poured from her mouth. This hair had covered one of her eyes in grammar school, as if protecting her from half the world.

"I . . . love you," she said to Hermes, or some indiscriminate person who was not there at all.

Hermes and I were unable to determine whom she had been speaking to, but rather than ask, we took her downstairs. She was too drunk to stand on her own, so we had to carry her over the narrow steps—a task that proved much harder than we had expected it to be.

I looked around for Antonia's parents on the second floor, but they were nowhere to be found. They must have left their worries for the next day, entrusting the rest of the house to their adorable cocker spaniel, who was sitting in the den, curiously watching our crash landing on a couch, barely managing to save Olivia. I went to fetch a glass of water for

Olivia. I was sure Antonia had told everyone the lower floors were off limits, but I did not think that she would mind. We were only taking care of a friend and would not allow the cancerous party to spread beyond the boundaries she had set. As I poured a glass of water from the bathroom's marble sink, I looked into the mirror again, wondering if I would ever hold a conversation with the other side. Then the cup began to overflow with cold water and I walked back to the den.

Olivia was sitting up now, wavering from side to side, mumbling now and then in obscure, confusing phrases that even she would not have understood if she had heard herself while sober. I put the water to her lips while Hermes told her it would help. She looked at both of us and blinked. Butterfly flapping its wings in slow motion—kaleidoscope patterns in strobe lights. Her watch reminded me of my own, which I did not have with me. I realized that I did not have my wallet either, or my keys—just my deck of cards.

She saw me looking at the watch and, in a slurred voice, said,

"Fuckin' Handcuff. That's why everyone has'm on their left hand. Even if you're a righty . . . don't understand it. Do you guys understand it?"

Hermes and I looked at each other's wrists. He had his watch on his right hand. And of course, I wasn't wearing one. Lore looked down as we looked up to her, letting our eyes roll along the luxurious curves of her body, so well defined by her tight black clothes. Upon her slightly tanned chest, a silver necklace made a path of liquid metal from her neck down to the top of her shirt, calling to attention the unknown regions of her cleavage and on throughout the valleys of her skin. A part of it was on her tongue, so that the trail lead up into her muddled mouth, where she was passing it from one cheek to the other, like waves inside a hidden cove. She saw our wrists and cursed, or rather spat through her vocal cords with no attempt at molding her self-disgust into cohesive words.

Although Olivia was a sorry sight to see, Hermes smiled and took her left hand in his own.

"You won't remember this tomorrow morning, because you're drunk, but all of us know that everything you see, no matter how messed up you are, goes somewhere in that mind of yours."

"So we're going to leave a message for you," I continued, "although you may not recall it tomorrow. But in some way or another, you will ultimately remember."

Hermes removed the watched and handed it to me. I took Olivia's right hand and clasped the watch, which I had removed from her left wrist.

Hermes spoke.

"The reason why you, and so many other people, are in such a state, is because you have no other way of communicating. We do drugs. We spend money. Our sense of love is profoundly impaired because we do not know how to communicate the essential messages of love that each of us contain within ourselves."

Hermes made her take another sip of water. She continued to drink as we talked.

"You're drunk right now. You aren't ready to understand this" I said, "but to tell you the truth, I'm so fucking confused about it right now I'm not even sure we're doing the right thing. But we have to make sure you'll be okay, and one day, when the time is right, you will wonder why you started wearing this on the other wrist, and you'll recall what we said."

I doubted whether we were right in assuming she would remember anything. The image of her eyes as butterflies was becoming distorted as her eyes began to role around. Now and then she would manage to focus—triggered, perhaps, by the tone of our voices. We paused and she managed to raise both her hands and place them on our cheeks.

"You guys're so cute. So cute. One a these days I'm just gonna call you up . . . outta the blue . . . talk to you, see how ya'll are doing. And we'll be friends again . . ."

I completed the sentence for her.

" . . . You'll think it's out of the blue, but in truth, you'll be remembering this moment."

She made a gesture, as if about to respond, but instead passed out, dropping her head onto my shoulder, breathing heavily, as if all we had done was catch her talking her sleep.

"Do you think she'll be alright?" I asked him.

"Yeah she'll be fine. She just had a long week."

I would like to have done something else for her—tell someone that she was sleeping in the den. But I was too afraid to climb the stairs again, and the room looked so comforting, I couldn't bare to think that someone might make her get up and sleep upstairs in some awful corner, surrounded by that false laughter and smoke. I imagined her waking up the morning after, wondering how she got there, forgetting the time we had spent together, oblivious of our discussion. Beams of light would spread diagonally from windows to the floor, illuminated by the particles of dust that floated through the air. She would wake up slowly, with a headache perhaps, wondering what had happened. And I had no idea where I would be when she woke up, but I hoped it would not be there. At least we had gotten her downstairs.

Hermes and I continued down the stairs and had our hands on the front door when I heard my name called from above. It was Antonia, calling from the fifth floor. I looked up through the middle of the spiral staircase. I could see all the way to the ceiling. Antonia's long black hair was tied back with a scarf, only allowing a single strand of hair to creep out and hang in my direction.

"Where are you going Phaedrus? Don't you want to stay a little longer?"

Although her face was the only thing I could see, it was enough to make my lips dry. Although my considerations of the night had been full of fear and disgust towards the party she was hosting, I felt a sense of acceptance from her stare. I thought about how much easier it would be to stay.

"Hermes has to go somewhere . . . he has to leave" I replied, shouting over the noise.

I had meant to reply stubbornly—to politely excuse myself—but my voice came out as if from the shadows of hesitancy. What young man has reason enough to deny the fruits that lay upstairs? Another face appeared on the fourth floor, where the library was. It was the same floor we had left Olivia to sleep on.

"Dumai, Phaedrus Dumai?"

He spoke in the same way his hair was slicked back and parted to the side—as if his hair-cut had a voice unto itself and the round, slightly pudgy face that curled around its words were merely there to hide this peculiarity. He slowly descended the stairs so that his head revolved around the borders of my vision, gradually growing and coming into focus. When he was finally standing at the steps in front of me, I saw that he was dressed in a white V-neck sweater and old-fashioned pants.

His overall impression—clothes, hair, ambience, the contours of his face—seemed so *vintage* that I doubt the kids upstairs had been able to mock him or even talk behind his back. He was at ease with himself, like nothing was wrong with his demeanor—as if everyone else was wearing a costume. He was the emperor, wearing the emperor's new clothes, only this time everyone could see what he was wearing.

"Yes" I said, "That's me."

I heard Hermes shuffle as if silently saying, 'I have to go'.

"You're father is Kyo Dumai, is he not?"

I nodded.

"Then that makes us mutual acquaintances, to quite a strange degree!"

He took the last step down in my direction so that we were finally level with each other. He affectionately placed his hand upon my shoulder. He had an old-fashioned tennis racket in his left hand—the kind with a wooden frame and brown leather grip.

"Our fathers were close friends at the University of Chili—very close friends if I recall correctly. Please, join us upstairs, won't you? The whole gang is in the den, and they'd just love to meet you. There's so much catching up to do!"

"Are you at the University of Chili too?" I asked. I wanted to know if there was any place in the world where people were still like him.

"Princeton, actually. So is everyone upstairs. Come on then, I'll introduce you."

"What about Antonia's party?"

He stepped very close to me, cupping the side of his mouth in order to tell a secret.

"Immature brats if you ask me," he whispered through the side of his mouth, "Don't worry, we can't hear them in the library."

I looked back up the stairs at Antonia, who hadn't moved.

"Phaedrus, meet Ashta."

Ashta instantly presented his hand for shaking as if the speed at which he did so would demonstrate the extent of his enthusiasm.

"Our families are close friends" Antonia continued, "I'll see you in the den after I kick these kids out."

Ashta patted me on the back and started pulling me upstairs.

"It's Ashta the second, to be precise, but everyone calls me Ash."

He leaped past me with his hand so that he stood before Hermes.

"And you must be Hermes! Antonia tells me you're also studying at UC? How spectacular! Please, join us!"

Before his indecisiveness looked rude, Hermes shrugged in a stoic manner and said, "Well, it's not as if the trains ever stop in New York. I don't mind staying a little longer."

"Marvelous!" Said Ashta.

It wasn't as if we were going back to the party, and Ashta's firm grasp on our shoulders made us feel welcome. I saw his shining teeth through a wide, Cheshire cat grin, making him seem so directly from the 1950's that I could not help my fascination. If our fathers had been friends—and

Ashta was the ideal model of my father's era—I was apt to learn a great deal about my father's past.

Up and around we went again, ascending the spiral staircase to the library. The music's hypnotic rhythms faded until Antonia, shouting everyone out of her house, was all we could hear. Hermes and I were ushered into a large old-fashioned library. There were four others—dressed like Ashta—laughing with similar grins at some joke we had missed. They were sitting around a chessboard that no one seemed to be playing, although its pieces were scattered around the board.[3]

"Great news chaps! I found Kyo's son, and his friend Hermes!"

"How enchanting!"

"Bravo, Ashta!"

"Three cheers!"

I caught a glimpse of Olivia before being pushed into the library. She was still sleeping soundly on the couch. One of Ashta's friends, who had bright blonde hair and tailored white slacks took an immediate interest in Hermes' name.

"Named after the myth, I presume?"

"I get that a lot. Actually, I am Hermes."

And then everyone laughed of course and another one of Ashta's friends, who had wrapped his white cotton sweater over his shoulders and tied the arms in a knot over his chest said "Sure, and I got into Princeton because of my academic record!"

And they all laughed like they were sitting in some country club. Hermes and I laughed too, although we didn't really find it that funny.

---

[3] The night before, Antonia's father, Michael, had been reading a letter from his friend Simon, requesting help on one of his stories. In it, a schizophrenic bachelor with a love for chess began playing a game via the post. Little did the man know, however, that he was actually playing the game of chess with his other personality. Simon was attempting to use the moves of the game to symbolize various elements of the tale, and wanted Michael's advice on how to proceed.

"I used to joke about it" Hermes continued after the laughing had faded to some extent, "but just the other day I woke up and realized that it was true." Everyone smiled, expecting some kind of punch line, except for me, who had no idea what he was talking about. There was something of an awkward pause while the climax everyone had been waiting for didn't happen, and the snazzy looking yuppies concluded he was either crazy or drunk. Probably the latter, because something made Ashta pick up a flask and offer drinks. I politely tried to decline when the flask came round to me, shaking my head with a smile.

"Oh come on now Phaedrus, we must make a toast—how often do you run into a piece of your father?"

This is how a glass of some strange drink that resembled Brandy ended up in my veins.

"To getting a glimpse of it all, right guys?" Ashta said, holding his glass into the circle we had made around the chess board.

"And grasping it too!" Said the blonde.

"And telling it to others." Hermes continued. Everyone looked at me, so I finished.

"And using it correctly."

"Cheers!"

And we drank.

And we drank and we drank and we drank. Antonia joined us at some point or another after she had cleaned up the mess from the party. Ashta told me about his father, so I told him about mine while the others listened, occasionally commenting with witty remarks. Although the weather was warm outside, a fire had been lit for atmosphere. Ashta and his friends attended Ivy league schools and came from prestigious families. They loved the fact that I was a performer. My card tricks sent them straight into hysterics.

"I wish I could perform" Ashta lamented once I had turned the blue cards back to red, "but I get such bad stage fright, I can't even order a value meal at Burger King without stumbling over my words."

This confused me. I don't know why.

"Oh, Ashta, don't tell me you go to Burger king!" exclaimed the boy with the sweater around his shoulders. Two red-heads with freckles and puffy cheeks, who were twins and apparently captain and co-captain of their school's championship polo teams, and who always carried their polo sticks with them wherever they went, simultaneously turned around and looked at the boy with the sweater.

"I think I speak for Marco too when I voice my disgust for anything BUT Burger King" The one on the right said.

The blonde boy interrupted,

"Are you all mad? Cheap corporate fast food? Now Wendy's? . . . *that's* a quality meal."

"I used to be a loyal McDonald's patron to tell you the truth," said Ashta, who had stood up and placed one leg up on the ottoman of the chair next to him, "but the flame broiled burger really does taste better."

"You're a traitor, Ash" Antonia said, hinting towards sarcasm, "will the Golden Arches ever let you come back?"

"Oh stop."

We all laughed. The twins had a wonderful way of laughing together—like singing in harmony. They crossed their arms and chuckled so their spotted cheeks expanded; two halves of a moon on each face, around freckles that could have been stars.

Ashta turned a log in the fire, and when I looked back at the others, I realized Hermes was gone. I felt somewhat irritated that he had not said goodbye, but assumed he had his reasons why.[4]

Antonia was on the couch between the blonde and the one wrapped up in a sweater, flirting with them, occasionally

---

[4] I did not discover where Hermes had gone for a very long time. I was sitting in a park one day and he was suddenly sitting there next to me, wearing a new pair of sneakers with some kind of white extensions attached at the sides. I asked him where he had gone that night and he told me that he hadn't really gone anywhere at all. It was one of the most important nights of his life—the night he rose to something greater. He tried to explain it to me, but the details were too complicated for me to understand. All I could gather was that it had had something to do with the Internet.

touching her shoulder or some other area of her body that would have normally seemed platonic. She winked at me. I smiled.

"That girl is lost" Ashta said, eyes still on the flames, poker in hand. I was sitting on the ottoman that should have been holding his feet.

"Why do you say that?"

"She's torn between a world of blissful ignorance and a much, much deeper part of existence."

"How?"

"Her family lineage is connected to a sacred order. But her beauty, her age, this city, and her avoidance of the truth is keeping her at bay from her destiny."

"That was pretty heavy Ashta, why are you telling me this? Are you trying to tell me something else? I hate it when people try to tell me something by saying another. Why not be straightforward?"

"Because truth can be brutal, and the soul is a sensitive entity. The truth, well, truth is like a good Medusa."

He took a sip of the Brandy-like liquid, poking the log for dramatic effect.

"Only we must use several mirrors. And truth is ultimately good, not evil. Once one defeats her—that is, really understands the truth—it can be used to stop evil. Stop fear. Stop ignorance in its tracks."

"You say you're in college . . . you and your friends. But you aren't are you? You're much older."

"And you give the impression of a naïve boy, Phaedrus. But you aren't, are you? It's just another one of your illusions. You want to make a difference, and that is good, but you think the way to do it is by using your mind. You must use your heart. Do not analyze so much. Not me. Not anything, because if you do, you'll find a maze too big. It will drive you crazy, like the scientists. Would you rather know how a magic trick works, or accept it as the miracle it appears to be?"

"Why do you think I became a magician?"

"Because you know it is necessary to make other people believe. Don't wizards say that the greatest miracles occur in the hands of the master who believes it himself?"

"We could talk forever like this."

"It's human nature."

"Circles."

"Yes, around and around, perpetually avoiding the most significant center that is responsible for all motion."

"Wow. I thought I was deep."

"That's why we met."

"Are you sure?"

"Positive."

"Explain."

"I don't have to. That's the point."

He stood up, crossed the room, and sat down near Antonia's devotees.

Five Days Later: Go to chapter 12
Five Decades Later: Go to chapter 5

Chapter 21

I was unable to make out her words before she finished saying them, but they had been loud enough to rise me from a strange dream, which evaporated from my memory as soon as I woke up. I opened my eyes and saw a Natalie that wasn't fully there. Only a fraction of her was present in the room—in transition, do doubt, between the world I had created and her own. I do not know exactly where she would end up, only that it took her *somewhere*, and the body she had once inhabited now lay upon the floor, completely empty of its soul (or, shall I say, the reflection of a soul).

Before her body had fallen down, I had opened my eyes in time to see her leaving. Although she did not move her hand, or even say goodbye, I knew that she was thinking thoughts of closure. Her body became impossible to distinguish between the space she had occupied and the physical material that she had consisted of, as if she had been made of transparent glass that, until now, had established an opaqueness by means juxtaposition with various angles of light.

The sensation of loss was far worse than if she had died, for in that moment I could no longer deny that she had never lived at all. Although I had managed to fool myself within my own illusion, there was no comfort in the thought that I had run away from solitude into a lover made of smoke and mirrors.

I sat up in my bed, kneeling at the other end, and looked onto the carpeted floor, where the rest of Natalie was vanishing. A few lights from the building next to ours were glowing through our bedroom window, so that her face became a disconnected field of geometric shapes make it impossible to see her as a whole.

A few seconds later, the light from outside was no longer on her face, but on the floor beside her, where it would have shined had her body not been there. When I looked back to see how the light was managing to shine through her, she was no longer there.

I stood up, leaning my forehead against the large glass window, through which I could see the city skyline. I considered jumping off the balcony.

Instead, I left the room and went out to the hall, carefully avoiding the walls of pictures, terrified of walking backwards through the discourse of my life. Convicted felons walking passed their victims and the media, head bowed down to block the world around as they approach the consequence of crimes committed.

In my study, I sat down at my desk and turned my picture frames downwards, afraid she might not be in them anymore. I had forgotten to turn my computer off. The small green light was still on. I thought about all the books I had written, wondering why, after all this time, I still used my old pseudonym, "Simon Cryptus." I had revealed my true identity so long ago, yet still refused to work under my real name. Was I obsessed with masks? Did I prefer to live behind my own creations?

Looking out the window, I saw something happening in the penthouse apartment a few buildings down the street. All of its lights were on, and many silhouettes were moving back and forth. I turned the computer off and walked over to the window. I unscrewed the ends of my telescope my father had given me for Christmas many years ago. I carefully adjusted the focus, positioning the telescope so I could see into the room. There was certainly some kind of party going on, although I could not make out the guests. A musician was playing frantically in the corner, while some people stood by the large, expansive windows that apparently made up the entire wall.

Zooming in, I realized they were looking into telescopes. Standing at the second one over from the musician, a strangely familiar figure seemed to have adjusted his telescope directly at my own. I tried to adjust the lens further, hoping to recognize him. But as I turned the lens, his figure did not become clearer, but rather the lens through which he was observing *me*.

The view became sharper, until eventually I could make out the details of his lens—surprised to find that I could actually see something at the center.

A room came into view that looked completely different from the penthouse. Initially, I thought it might be the reflection of my own study in his telescope, but this was not the case. It was a bedroom, with windows looking into a tree. A child's room—glowing stars had been stuck on the ceiling and posters taped onto the wall.

Suddenly, I knew why the details of the room were so vivid. I had been there before. It was my own room. I had grown up in it, and although the picture was a bit distorted by the lens, I felt as though time had never played its course on me at all.

Go To chapter 0

Chapter 12

I decided to walk home. For once in my life I was dressed for the cold. New York City was near freezing, but my jacket and the night's bizarre memories were enough to keep me warm. Although Manhattan never sleeps, it certainly gets quiet at three in the morning on the Upper East Side. The few people I saw while walking uptown seemed anxious to get back inside. However, I felt rather disappointed when I got home. I stood under the awning of the building, waiting for the doorman to wake up and let me in. After one last look at an empty Fifth Avenue, covered by traffic lights without any cars to stop, I waited for the door to open.

Once I was inside, the doorman gave me a dreary nod before he made his way back to the couch, as if still inside his dream. The lobby resembled the basement of a gothic church, with dark brown stones and doorways shaped like bishop's hats.

I turned into a dark hallway, walking towards the elevator. As soon as I saw the tall brass doors of the lift, the sense of contentedness that I had brought home with me gave way to dire emptiness. Never had I felt so lonely, for it seemed as though the magic had departed, not even leaving me with someone else to talk about it with. The loneliness increased each time I stepped forward, so that by the time I reached those doors, I was praying for someone to appear behind them. I cannot say the feeling was a bad one though. Everyone indulges in self-sympathy from time to time. I would even say that it is somewhat therapeutic. I paused before pushing the button. I hoped that I might find the answer to my solitude behind the doors. I realized my eyes were closed. I opened them and saw my finger hesitantly hovering before the button. A heavy breath, and then I pushed.

The button flashed and the doors parted. My eyes desperately searched the interior, and caused my heart to flood with blood by the recognition of a moving, breathing, human being. But the elevator was empty—all I had seen was my reflection in the elevator's mirrors. I sighed and stepped inside. I turned around and listened as my breath returned to normal. I ran my hands along the soft red velvet walls. I let my long black hair surround my eyes, allowing it to envelop my empty stare.

I was attempting to cocoon myself in solitude when she called out loud to hold the elevator. I jerked my head up in surprise and blocked the closing doors. I managed to produce a decent smile. I did not look at her. Instead, I chose to keep my head bowed, seeing nothing but the shoes she wore as she crossed over the polished floor and on into the lift. The doors were shutting as she slipped inside, so that by the time she reached me, they had closed completely.

Elevator etiquette is all too much a part of life. We do not enter them and stare at one another. We turn around and look at the display, or the floor, or our nails, or a magazine. Nevertheless, I allowed myself a glance in her direction. The top of her head was all I had to see (I assume she had been examining my shoes) to know that she was beautiful. It was the way her eyebrows arched towards her nose, and the elegance with which she moved her head upon the axis of her neck while tilting upwards to return my gaze. The last thing I heard from the lobby was the doorman, snoring.

Oh shit, I thought, *it's Natalie Portman.*

And by that time the doors had closed completely, and I had pressed the seventh button, and she had pressed the sixth. I decided not to say anything. I figured it best to keep silent, rather than stumble over words and make a fool out of myself. At least, this is what I thought until the lift stopped suddenly, causing both of us to stumble. We looked up towards an alarming sound of breaking gears and cables. Eventually, the tiny room fell silent and the shaking stopped.

Miyamoto Musashi was the greatest samurai warrior that ever lived. He wrote a book on strategy, and in it, stated that if one desired to win a battle, he must let his enemy strike first. Of course, Ms. Portman was no enemy, but I felt quite intimidated, and decided to wait until she said something first. Perhaps she was thinking along the same lines, unsure of what to say in such a situation, knowing that whatever happened would be remembered.

She sighed with frustration and cursed. Her purse jerked back and forth as she angrily shook about the tiny space. She almost stomped on the floor, then thought better of it. Trying my best to appear calm, I opened the cabinet containing the emergency phone and pressed the button inside as she watched. It was a look of involuntary concentration, the kind we get when caught off guard.

"Shoot, he's sleeping, isn't he?" she said, in reference to the doorman.

I nodded my head, listening to the phone. I envisioned the lobby, completely empty save the dull buzz of our phone as the doorman kept on sleeping and did nothing but incorporate the sound into his dreams.

We stood there waiting till my legs began to hurt and I sat down with the receiver. I kept my head to the wall, trying not to look at her. She kept on standing. By then, her purse was motionless. I took my eyes off the wall to look at her. She seemed transfixed by the phone, unwilling to our situation. Noticing the opportunity, I slowly let the phone hang by the plush red wall, so that its ringing was still audible, but barely so, and carefully spoke.

"No answer."

She sighed again, in a way that brought her shoulders to her head, then back down to the pockets of her black, tailored pants. With stunning elegance, she sank into an Indian's position and began to talk. I was not prepared for this. I could barely keep up. It was as though she had been mute for her entire life until that moment. Each thought she voiced flowed on into another, reminding her of something else she wanted me to know. I listened. I laughed. I sighed with sadness when it seemed appropriate. I thought to myself, 'I have done the same thing before, I have unloaded in this way. The proper thing to do is listen.'

Finally, she paused. Searching for her breath and trying to find something else to say, she looked at me. Another monstrous sigh, then, "I'm sorry. I don't mean to burden you like this, it's just that this entire circumstance is so bizarre."

I said something stupid, she told me to call her by her first name.

One way conversation turned into a dialogue, and for another length of time we swapped perspectives. I have never spoken so well. It felt as though my mind had acted instinctively, just as our bodies do in an emergency, putting every available effort into finding the right thing to say. Having succumbed to the heat by then, our apparel was strewn about the floor. The small room had become our own. She kept on mentioning the oddness of such circumstances, and each time I replied by curling my soft black hair around my fingers and expressing my stubborn belief that everything will happen for a reason, that coincidence does not exist.

Deeper and deeper we went into our introspection till neither of us were able to discern who we were talking about. She emptied the contents of her purse. I figured this to be some sort of climax, for no matter how far women go in trusting other men, purses are perpetually private. Yet she showed no hesitation when she swung the bag around and let a waterfall of personal possessions fall onto the carpet. She shifted through them one by one, narrating the story of each. There were addresses and make-up, pencils and pens, Broadway tickets and VIP passes. Then, finally, a strange lacquer box that resembled a miniature treasure chest. She picked it up and passed it in-between her hands.

"My grandmother's cook gave this to me. Told me to hold on to it. Told me that if God had the whole world in his hands, then someone was holding God too, and on and on, never ending."

"Like microcosms of microcosms."

The more I looked at it, the more enticing it became. A treasure chest that had never been buried or stowed away, but rather hidden in the most ingenious way: putting it where everyone can see it, so that no one would think twice. I wondered how many secrets there were that I would never know about—was there a finite number?

She flipped its clasp and opened it. It began to play music, a melody I recognized, but could not place exactly. I asked her what the tune was.

"Lakmé—Delibes. That Cook sure loved opera. I think her name was Thelma."

The music enchanted me so thoroughly that for a while I didn't even notice the two porcelain figures that slowly revolved around each other in the box, which was lined with soft red fabric. They were not dancers, yet dressed formally—as if waiting for the next waltz, or for the intermission to end in the lobby of a Broadway show.

"Beautiful, isn't it?"

I wanted to tell her how enchanting it was, but then the doors abruptly opened, revealing half of the sixth and seventh floor. I could see part of my mother's apartment above us, and what must have been Ms. Portman's below, separated by a thick black slab of scaffolding.

She sighed with relief, then looked at me.

"You're place or mine?" I said, trying to sound comical.

Seventh floor: Go to chapter 3.14
Sixth floor: Go to chapter 83

Chapter 83

I lowered myself onto her polished marble floor. It would have been a rather amusing sight, no doubt, for anyone entering the foyer at that moment. I made it to the ground and had Natalie in my arms when Domino ran into the foyer. Natalie immediately recognized his heavy footsteps and asked for his assistance. He heaved a sigh, adjusting his massive body and joined me in the awkward task of lowering her from the faulty elevator. Once we were all on safe ground, she introduced me to the butler.

Domino stopped fixing the bow tie on his tuxedo in order to shake my hand, completely engulfing my own with his massive fingers. He let go of my hand just moments before I thought it might pop and took Ms. Portman's coat. There was an awkward pause, and then my strange experience became nothing more significant than a large, retired object in the attic of my mind. Something put away and easily forgotten, only considered during infrequent visits to such places of inconvenient things.

Time seemed to pass, in the manner of a sound we do not hear because of its monotony. We wrapped golden rings around each other's fingers and to share a bed felt strange no longer.

Go on to the next page

Chapter 11

There was a night that would have been no different from the nights that came before it, if Natalie had not awoken in the middle of the night. She tossed and turned, but could not find her sleep again. It was cold outside and yet her perspiration caused everything to stick. The sheets were damp wet chains or, better yet, entangling pythons. With her head upon her elbow, she looked at me and at the digital clock. Both motionless. Both oblivious to Natalie's inspection. She began to play games with the numbers of the clock—math games that no one finds amusing, which we only utilize in times of extreme boredom. She thought it strange that five and seven made thirteen—that three and eight was only eleven. Shouldn't it be more?

She considered a pill. Television. But then her lover began to mumble in his sleep. She touched my lips as they moved, reminding her of spinning clay. I began to speak cohesively. I grew louder, as if irritated.

"Don't take me for a fool doctor. I know what is real and what is not."

She felt embarrassed, thinking that perhaps she should not be hearing this. The thought that lovers have no secrets quickly justified her apprehension though, and she continued listening.

"I come to you for help, not insults. What do you think I'm really doing if not sitting here in your office? Do you think I am a sleeping butterfly? Or perhaps I fell in love with a famous movie actress and married her, and just happen to be dreaming about the shrink I went to as a young man. No doc, I know when I am dreaming and I know when I'm awake, so please don't waste our time together like this. . . ."

Unable to listen any longer, Natalie left our bedroom. She walked along the hall, lined with pictures of her face on magazines and movie posters. Pictures of me signing books for presidents and popes. Pictures of us, together—wedding photographs, posters of movies we had made together. A hallway that traced our lives together. It had gone by so fast, she thought, *could* it be real?

Ice into a tumbler and the rare elixir I had introduced her to. Imported from some place she'd never heard of. It was only for special occasions—nostalgia and deep thoughts.

However, she found her memory unusual. She could not recall the details of our home, although it had belonged to us for many years. As though her memory was a house unto itself, she had no trouble recalling its basic layout. What disturbed her was her recollection of specific things—each time she thought about something in particular, it came indirectly, like inventing or guessing and finding such creations to be the actual recollection.

Her logical half said the drink was working fast, but the rest of her had already started exploring the idea that she was part of someone's dream. Like the man she had married, Natalie was creative in nature. Nevertheless, both of us enjoyed the harmony of logic and creativity. In this way, Natalie considered her existence.

After contemplating her position, she came to no conclusions whatsoever. What would happen when I woke up? If she was just a segment of my dreams, was she really thinking for herself? After a second glass of elixir, Natalie was basking in mysterious thoughts. If she stopped thinking, would she no longer exist? Good thing she had never tried meditation. Did these thoughts negate Descartes?

Miss Natalie Portman stood up—rather unsteadily however, due to her overindulgence in elixir—and made her way into the kitchen. She had always felt comforted by kitchens. A place where all inhabitants of a home are eventually present in, yet rarely leave a trace that they were there. Thus the sterile tile and linoleum floors are always clean on the surface, and yet the room is full of reminiscent feelings that remind one of their individual existences.

She poured some milk into a pan and turned the stove on. She did not think that it would help her sleep, but she found a sense of calm in ritual—doing something that has been done so many times.

Kitchens pleased her because they seldom had mirrors. Never being surprised by her own reflection made it possible to sink into that side of her that went beyond the physical. In the same way scents and tastes provided by a kitchen can solidify emotion.

Her stubbornness had done many different things for her throughout the course of her life. If the internal strife between existence and non-existence that she had only recently encountered was going to be her greatest challenge yet, her stubbornness would no doubt play a major role in the conclusion. The question was whether it would help or hurt her.

When the milk was warm enough, she put it in a glass and began to clean the pan she had used. As she poured liquid Joy into the sink, already half-full of water from the faucet, she considered the implications that her discoveries had presented.

If she was Natalie within the future kitchen of her lover's mind, and held onto her own existence with her stubbornness, what part of his mind did she really represent? Perhaps her stubbornness was merely an obsession that the man whose dreams encircled her was trying to let go of?

The pot in the sink was now overflowing with Joy, so she quickly finished her glass of milk and cleaned that too. When the dishes were done she confidently returned to the room and positioned herself at the foot of our bed.

"I will not be stubborn anymore, I am no longer a part of you" She said to me, "We are pieces of each other. Even if I don't exist right here, I must exist somewhere."

Go to chapter 21

"I am not a part of you," she said, "nor are we pieces of each other, you will no longer control my existence."

Go to chapter 96

Chapter 3.14

I walked silently through my apartment, knowing its layout so well that I did not need light. Pondering this thought, I grew somewhat distressed. Perhaps it is these times when one does not need light that bad things can happen. I skipped over certain steps in the staircase that would have made noise under my weight. I was standing in the middle of my room.

The bedroom had belonged to my brother, Ronin, before he had left to find himself in California. He had covered the ceiling with stars, so that when the lights were off, the room became its own universe. I wondered if perhaps stars shined because it was their only purpose—defining the universe by lighting it up—and when it could shine no longer, the absence of light caused the universe to collapse upon itself.[5] If I no longer needed any kind of light to walk through my apartment, or any area of my life, was I about to fall into infinity?

I stood under my universe within the universe and walked over to the window. I drew the curtains to the sides, deciding that if that was all there was to the cosmos, then I probably *was* in some kind of black hole. I waited for a gust of wind to push the tree aside, curious to see if anyone I knew was out there.

Go to chapter 0

[5] See Illustration 8

Chapter 96

Natalie grew more confident as she said these words. In her stubbornness, she realized that her creator was no longer relevant, as birds that leave their nest and children who become independent. As she thought about this to herself, the sleeping body started losing its shape and form, like an optical illusion that fooled her no longer.

She was not happy doing this, it did not give her any pleasure; more like suddenly realizing that something must be done. Like ending a relationship that had started to smell, and had only managed to live so long because its ingredients could not bear to end something that had been so good.

The world became her own. She was free to create and destroy. She created the death of her lover who, in actuality, had simply left the reality he had forged for them. But she mourned as if he actually died, using her period of isolation to compose the boundaries of her starveling universe.

She had not expected this process to be so challenging. Now that it was possible to have anything she wished for, she had to find out what she wanted. This was surprisingly harder than finding out how to get what she needed—she no longer needed anything at all.[6]

She decided to have a child. It would not be a normal child though—she wanted a child with magic in its veins, so that they could mold their universe together. What she did not know, however, was that by summoning a magical father rather than creating one, her universe would no longer completely belong to her.

But when her doorbell rang unexpectedly one day, she knew that she had done the right thing. In a world where nothing happened unless she created it, the unexpected had

---

[6] Once, Natalie tried to imagine the most extravagant luxury possible, and instantaneously found herself beside an Olympic sized pool, filled to the brim with Don Perignon. She had swum two lengths and came out of the pool so tipsy that the servants had to help her out.

never existed. Lying in the entrance of her home there was an antique oil lamp, without any hint as to who it could have come from. As one might expect, this lamp had not materialized for the sole purpose of illumination. It also contained the genie that, eventually, gave her twins—a boy and a girl.

Natalie never lived an unsurprising day again.

Go to Part II

Chapter 50

I was surprised to see you when I turned around. No doubt you were as well, for until then it was only vaguely apparent that you had anything to do with this story. You had considered yourself an objective observer—the natural position of any reader. But there you were with me, standing on the dock that looked exactly as you had imagined it, watching Bobby push away and sail into the distance. You knew for certain that before arriving, a sense of confusion had lingered in your mind. However, these feelings of bewilderment no longer mattered. Your sudden confrontation with the vision of the sailing boat and me, the writer of the very story you were reading, made you feel much better.

And I have to say the same went for myself. Before that moment, I did not know whom I had been telling my story to. Seeing you in person seemed to justify my work. You wrapped your arms around your body as you walked over the planks towards me. The sound of waves eventually faded until the repetition turned to nothing more than soothing background noise.

My line of vision swayed between you and the sea's horizon, which stretched so far it bent according to the roundness of the world. As you approached me, you saw that I was smiling. We sat down on the planks and let our legs swing over the edge. When I spoke, it felt like a comfortable act of progression, not some social attempt to fill the emptiness between us. Before we had been sitting there, I wasn't sure that everything was making sense, I could not describe it to myself, let alone another person, but I put myself into your shoes and spoke as if speaking to myself.

"You are here because right now you don't know where you are."

I smiled a bit more, then shrugged. "Hey, to tell you the truth, I don't know why I'm here either. One moment I was hanging with my friends outside the Metropolitan, and the next, I was here. All I know is that we can help each other out, because we are both in need of direction."

I hesitated a moment, looking into the overcast sky, still smiling.

"Well, not exactly direction . . . more like a better understanding of the direction we're already taking."

I nodded at you, as though agreeing with myself, content with my attempt to clarify things for us both.

I stood up, still smiling, then turned around and walked towards the edge of the dock. I knew, somehow, that I would not fall into the water. It seemed appropriate to you as well, and when we looked around again, we found that we were in a different place entirely. You were sitting at a giant table, and everyone you knew was there as well. Although it might have seemed a little strange in such a place, there it was—hard oak, circular, straight out of the dining room you always thought about when visions of a family life passed through your head. It was a large room. A penthouse apartment perhaps, where some kind of reception was being held. You realized that the music you heard was coming from the corner, where bobby was doing his thing on an elevated stage. Gigantic windows were displaying the New York City skyline, and several telescopes had been lined up the glass.

Your oldest friend from nursery school, who you hadn't spoken to in years, sat beside your father. At the other end, smiling across the reflective surface, sat the high school love that broke your heart—the one that took you so long to forgive. Your favorite relatives were there, gossiping about the family. Everyone was smiling. Although you knew that they were there for you, you did not feel selfish—they talked and laughed with one another. Everyone you ever cared about had finally received a chance to meet—to share stories of you. To celebrate life with you.

No one seemed unhappy with the temperature in there. Those who liked the fall wore sweaters and long pants, and those in preference of warm weather donned summer slips and sunglasses. It was most definitely night, although each face you studied seemed directly in a ray of light. Your favorite meal was being served; everyone ate off of porcelain plates.

Your closest friend shook hands with the teacher that changed your life, and then you saw that I, too, was there, standing the same distance from you as I had on the dock, in the middle of the room.

I turned away and waved to the high-school love. I exchanged formalities with your oldest of relatives (who died a few years back). The teacher that made such a difference must have said something humorous, for when I heard the whisper in my ear, I started laughing loudly. I slowly turned my gaze to you again, and mentioned how becoming your attire was.

"But of course, we haven't come this far to tell you what you know already."

My voice seemed to echo, as if I were lip-synching.

"People think God, or the answer, or whatever you want to call it, lies somewhere in the clouds. 'The heavens', they say. They feel depressed when they perceive their path as flat, rather than inclined towards that special place above. They do not feel that they are getting closer, because they do not think that they are moving upwards. Little do they know that the answer has no destination, for it is infinite, and the paths that lead into the sky stretch on into eternity. Thus, we do not perceive an incline at all on our path—it seems completely flat. We do not see our continual progression towards this higher place that every person ultimately seeks."[7]

I sunk into my seat. You looked around again. The ones who raised you were conversing with your heroes, nodding their heads in agreement. Everyone was taking pictures of each other—putting on their Kodak smiles and interlocking arms; the confrontations that you never thought would happen were recorded by the flashing lights that somehow seemed to lighten up the room in streams of slow, surreal snapshots.

---

[7] See Illustration 7

"So when you think that you aren't going anywhere, remember what I said here." I placed my hand on your shoulder.

"In the end, everyone is moving upwards, and the only thing to fear is backward motion, or convictions that we aren't getting closer to the sky."

I stopped talking and smiled. I kept my hand upon your shoulder. I turned back to the gathering and then, just as smoothly as you had come into the story, you vanished from the contents of these sentences, leaving me with your memories and mine. Because I did not really know anyone at the party, I decided to inspect the telescopes. Signs had been attached to the tripods. I approached the closest one and read the writing, which was printed in blue ink.

TELESCOPE #1
JUST A GLASS OF WATER
The future of Rain and Sammy Aldo

TELESCOPE #2
TODAY AND TOMORROW
A retrospective

I smiled and went on without stopping.

TELESCOPE #3
TWO LOVERS
One sleeping, one awake

TELESCOPE #4
PENELOPE
Subject of considerable remorse for Bobby Snaplett, tonight's guest musician.

TELESCOPE #5
ISIT AND ITIS
The twin brother and sister of a genie

Telescope #1 Go to chapter 29
Telescope #2 Go to chapter 5
Telescope #3 Go to chapter 11
Telescope #4 Go to chapter 601
Telescope #5 Go to chapter 609

Chapter 601

Alice and Penelope Eve were sitting in a large, elaborate room. Servants had served them tea. The air was conditioned appropriately. Penelope's hair was straight yet voluminous. She sat upon a stool before her vanity mirror, so she could see herself from various angles. If there was a name for women such as Penelope, it would be 'killer butterfly,' because although her dapper eyes could fly and taunt each person that she fluttered by, there was a sting that came each time she landed. It was this aspect of danger that made one feel self-conscious when they walked in her vicinity.

She was applying eye shadow. Alice sat in the other corner, watching. The room appeared to be dark because there were no bright colors inside. It was a serious room, where serious ideas were thought and serious dreams were seriously considered. She was telling Alice about her childhood. Her hair had been long when she was young. Her father—a rocket scientist for NASA—liked it braided. He made sure not to lose her by holding her hair when they walked through crowds, like torturous reigns that reminded her of a bull's nose ring. Although it was extremely painful for Penelope, it worked extremely well. Penelope hated the way she was treated. When she was old enough, she cut off her hair and put it in a box with a note for her father, telling him that she was leaving. She did not let her hair grow back for fifteen years, and had only just begun to grow it out again.

She was an opera singer. The contents of her vanity table were scattered over sheets of music. Black pens lied amongst her make-up. Alice did little more than sit there in her large old-fashioned dress. There was a distinct contrast between Alice's dark hair and Penelope's. Alice had an ornate tiara holding back her hair, slightly stretching her wrinkles towards her hairline, providing the illusion that there were no wrinkles at all—strands of hair had merely fallen from beneath her headband. Thus, one could see the child she had been—innocent and curious, timid and naive. While

Penelope built up a barrier between her real face and the world with make-up and perfume, the only mask that Alice wore was age. She corresponded with the child that she had been so well this age became transparent—just another way to show the jubilance of simple-hearted people. She took the brush and started stroking Penelope's hair.

"The most poetic thing my father ever did," Penelope said to Alice, who did not have to turn around because they could see each other through the mirror, "Was put a compass on a necklace and send it to me with a note that said 'come back to me.'"

Alice slowed her brushstrokes down then stopped completely. She took out the brush and looked in the mirror. Penelope attempted to ignore the stare by picking up a pen and looking at a piece of music. She hummed enchantingly, like some romantic snake charmer. Killer butterflies have ways of hypnotizing any threat to its survival. Penelope's soprano melodies could stop a foe who put her lies in jeopardy.

"When will you finish your opera, Penelope? When will it be ready for the world to see?"

Alice did not appear desperate. It sounded like a practiced conversation, as if had been resurfacing for a very long time now.

"Nothing can wait forever Penelope. You just want to give up so you don't have to care. You told Bobby you would think about it once your opera was complete, so you don't complete your opera in order to ignore your heart. You refine and refine and if you go on like this you will no longer recognize your own creation."

Penelope sighed deep into her melancholy. Her body ran away from posture, meticulously sinking backwards throughout the impasse. She eluded Alice's gaze again by looking at her music—music she had looked at so many times she could hear the melodies within her head as soon as she saw the first bar of the page.

Alice and Penelope had planned on going to a costume party that night, but when she heard that Bobby would be playing there, she refused to go. Alice was still in her costume, wearing Red Ruby slippers for her Wizard of Oz costume.

In the end, it was not Alice's repeated appeals that made Penelope weary of her decision to stay home. While looking over her music, she had suddenly recalled a dream from several nights ago. In this dream, she had become a famous opera singer and Bobby had become a famous artist. Before one of her performances, he had come with flowers to see her, but she had not recognized him before waking. The dream made her realize that if it was not for Bobby, she never would have written the opera. However, if she did not deal with the romantic matter at hand with him, the opera would not only be about fear and despair—surely a good thing for any opera—but would also be born from these emotions. She could not allow this to happen.

Fear was thus the only thing that kept her from a wonderful party. A party that could make both of them happy. Fear was inhibiting not only herself but her dear friend Alice, and if it was possible to negatively influence another by your personal fears, how many had she already hurt because she could not confront love's uncertainties?

She shivered under Alice's comb, feeling the physical affects of despair in her skipping heart and dizziness. Therefore, Alice and Penelope rushed to the party—for Bobby, for the opera, but most importantly, for happiness. If there were any cabs to catch, they would only be fashionably late.

Go to Part II

Chapter 112263

"No" Said Constantine, "She's just a star I'll have to watch from here. I cannot reach that high yet."

Rain said nothing—nor did she move—just stood there with her eyes on Constantine. How long had she been standing like that? I am sure Alexander was wondering the same thing. I myself turned around and watched the mail girl walk away. The charts and graphs and monitors began turning themselves off. She let her feet drag, trying to leave a trail.

Constantine walked under the skeletal bones of his roof through the gigantic living room and looked out onto his backyard. A vast lawn, anointed by a pond in the shape of a thin moon, fell out from his back porch, as if his beautiful house had purged its inner self onto the world. We followed him outside and sat on the wicker furniture. Rain did not rock in her rocking chair. Constantine strummed his guitar while Alexander sipped his cancerous smoke.

Our exit was more graceful than our entrance had been. Rain stood up like she was leaving from a party that she no longer wished to attend and Alexander followed. They did not seem eager to accompany me. Perhaps Constantine had let them down. Alexander was ordering a cab and Rain had her eyes fixed on the driveway. When I started to make my way over to the pool house, which, amusingly enough, was in the shape of an over-sized dollhouse, she waved to me. I knocked on the door. It swung inwards. I was thinking about the gingerbread house in that fairy tale, but the image was distorted by loud music from within

It was Flamenco guitar—and yet accompanied by a clarinet, or could it be a saxophone? A whole band playing. But there was only one musician when I entered, strapped down by at least six instruments. He had short puffy hair and thickly framed glasses—a teenaged Woody Allen, but surely more attractive. He was crying, but not so loud that he did not hear my entrance.

The interior went well with my first impression of an oversized dollhouse. The furniture was child-sized, so Bobby was hunching in his leather chair and I was forced to squat in the alcove of the window, beside a miniature globe.

He was talented, no doubt. So talented in fact that I felt guilty about being his only audience. When his playing ended there was an immense, remorseful emptiness that fell over the room. A silence that longed for the music to come back and replace it. A silence reluctant to be there at all.

I put my hand upon the globe and rolled it back and forth in my hands.

"I'm in love with a girl named Penelope Eve and she loves me too." He said.

"Wonderful. Why don't you write a song for her?"

"Oh the song is where the tragedy begins Mr. . ."

"Dumai, Phaedrus Dumai."

He put his mouth on the clarinet and blew a melody that made the birds outside respond. His music felt differently when he played with his eyes open. Could it be compared with the mistake some people make of keeping their eyes open when they kiss for the first time? Does music seem more touching when musicians keep their eyes closed, because listeners feel like secrets are being revealed? I could not keep my own eyes open when he played with them shut—I would have felt intrusive. Like accidentally walking in on someone without clothes.[8]

"She tells me she's writing an opera, and can't think about anything else until it's finished. She thinks artists cannot love a person more than their art, so surely I can't really love her if I'm a musician, and how can she love me if her

---

[8] I brought this up with Bobby at a later date, and he told me an interesting story. He had played with Paul Desmond in Montego Bay for a few months, and said that audience members would occasionally see Mr. Desmond raising his eyebrows in a strange smile during sets. At first, Bobby had made the same mistake that the audience had made in assuming this quirky expression had something to do with his playing. As Bobby became more in touch with Desmond's style however, he realized that Desmond was actually smiling to different members in his band whenever they did something he liked.

opera means so much? I think she's just afraid of loving something that loves her back . . . isn't that what every artist is afraid of? They love their art and the relationship is defined much clearer in their hearts, because artists are born as artists, but no one is born a lover. You have to learn that the hard way."

I looked out the window, which appeared to be made of fiberglass so that it could not break and cut someone. There was a mini-bar where the real fridge would have been. A basket on the table had been filled with miniature fruit.

"I've got a gig in Manhattan tonight. I'm thinking maybe I should tell her the truth if she's there."

"Which is?"

"That both of us are right. I love her and we love our music. She's an opera singer and I found her through her voice while passing through the music building of a conservatory. She was singing—so beautifully I became frozen."

I wanted to now why we were sitting in a dollhouse, and what his connection with Constantine was. I could not find an opening to ask.

"This gig I have," he said, "I have a weird feeling about it. It's for some weird party on the river. A bunch of people I've never heard of. I'm going any moment now. Do you want to come? It's some kind of costume party . . . either way, there's nothing really going on out here."

Bobby stood up from a floor of instruments. There were banjos and harmonicas, flutes and violas. Even a long metal saw. He was wearing leather pants that must have been Italian, like some sort of junkie who cannot afford to concentrate on style, so bought whatever seemed luxurious and fell into them when it seemed appropriate. Truckers on long hauls. Cowboys who make up that rustic look without any effort. He noticed me staring.

"Do I fit some kind of stereotype? Maybe that's why Penelope doesn't want a musician. Maybe that's why she thinks we're all the same, and maybe because she's a musician herself, she's afraid of loving herself . . . and doesn't an artist have to be humble? Once an artist loses his humility, he becomes some sort of icon, some kind of fad that's been produced."

"Perhaps you're having trouble defining the line between self-confidence and arrogance," I said. But he hadn't heard me at all. He had not completed his thought.

"Maybe she feels adulterous, because she loves her music so much, like some passionate adultery of spirits, as if I might be unfaithful to her in the way she is unfaithful to me when lost within some aria."

There was a grandfather clock by the plastic wall, swinging back and forth. They are called grandfather clocks because such men know time too well. In too much wisdom they regress from worlds they've had enough of. How many times would Bobby hear the garbled talk of Eve's distorted clock? I wondered if Bobby's grandfather clock would sound like a normal clock, or if its sound would be closer to that of a host who strikes his spoon against a glass.

It was six minutes to nine. Soon enough, the bell would toll for me. Bobby had started to change into a white tuxedo, cautiously stepping through his sea of instruments. I wondered how he planned on carrying them. When he finished getting ready, he put them in the appropriate cases, which were all lined with velvet in various dark hues, and strapped them over his shoulder with some kind of grace that resembled a jester. Like professional jugglers handling two balls. Just playing another instrument.

"Let's go," he said, "before the tide changes."

I followed him out the back door onto wooden platforms that rested on a series of dunes. There was a breeze in the air that smelled like the sea, followed by my sudden apprehension of humidity. There was probably some kind of water on the other side. Bobby had already reached the highest part of the planks, so I rushed across the wood in order to catch up. The wooden platform reached past the sandy hill and over the water, supported by tall thin beams. There was certainly some kind of beach that joined the water and the dunes, but we certainly weren't on the ocean.

Bobby was loading his instruments into a boat at the end of the platform, beginning to untie thick ropes that looked older than the boat. The boat itself looked like a larger version of those origami vessels one makes out of newspapers as a child, only much larger, and of a plausible design. Perhaps it was old gray paint that looked like newspaper, or some strange design of Bobby's.

I stopped on the platform, between the dunes and Bobby's boat. Watching Bobby load his instruments caused me to think about how strange his world was in comparison to mine and the uncanny circumstances that had taken me thus far. There had been so many choices in so short an expanse of time, like Alice in her Wonderland, or my own private odyssey through the dreams of an opium smoker. How many times, I wondered, had I been brave enough to take a chance? A risk? Looking back on things, I realized that acting logically in such an illogical world as this one made *me* the crazy one. I had tried to be cautious, yet each time things had only gotten stranger. But nothing bad had happened. It felt so *easy*.

"Is there something wrong," Bobby asked, untying the final rope, which he had managed to pry open with his fingers. It had been a tight one, which is probably why he had decided to untie it last, "or are you just reflecting for a moment?"

I wanted to say both, but I suddenly became aware of someone else's presence behind me. The planks of wood were bending underneath the extra pressure. Bobby put the knot down (which he had almost defeated) and approached me.

"I think I understand what's troubling you."

"You do?" I replied. I got the sense that I should not turn around yet to see who was behind me, that I should wait to see what Bobby had to say.

"The way I see it, there is a point of no return for every journey, and it is resting on the fulcrum that supports the bridge one walks across. Like a see-saw. Scientists study the smallest elements of the universe by blowing them up. These elements resemble solar systems and other elements of space that are incomprehensibly larger than us. I'm sure you know this already . . . old advice, no? Perhaps though, you are merely in the middle of your experience—upon the fulcrum, or the point of no return. One event caused an explosion of separate events, of alternate realities, and you are merely in one part of it—one section of the element a scientist explodes for study. You should not feel weary of this, because after something breaks, one has the opportunity to do something not even the scientists are capable of doing."

"Which is?"

"Putting it back together. Up down, left right, love fear. Everything operates in waves . . ."

I was relieved to hear him mention waves, because it made me think that we were at least using some familiar point of reference. Perhaps he was just expanding on it. Or simplifying it.

" . . . Perhaps you are on some wave, a special wave perhaps, or a common one. When in the middle of a wave, you are no higher or lower than you were when you started or you finished. Like two people switching places on the end of a seesaw by running across."

"Like the fulcrum?"

"Precisely. So you got here from there, which was the same place as here, but in a way that is unlike the next part of the ride, which will ultimately lead you to the same place. You perhaps feel a little strange about being here, but now you must decide how you to return. I myself must go now, for just as the tides are shifting in your own waves, they are shifting in the waters below us.

"You know what's behind you" he said, pointing over my shoulder, "But you do not know what lies behind *me*. You can take a chance and come with me, or go back. It is your choice."

With that, he untied the final knot and jumped into his boat.

Go With Bobby: Go to chapter 666

Find Out Who Is Behind Me: Go to chapter 50

Chapter 100

I made my way towards the door. Although I had no desire to look Sammy in the eye I forced myself to keep my head up, watching him as I crossed the room. With a polite bow, Sammy kept his fists loosely curled at his sides, implying that I was welcome to proceed.

"What about Dr. Chambers?" I asked.

"He's going to stay with me, so I can provide him with further technical information regarding this wonderful machine of his."

Dr. Chambers appeared to be himself once more—emotionless, calm, and eager to take on the task at hand. He appeared as confident as he usually did, which made me realize he had probably never been as confident as I thought.

Alexander and Rain did not seem ecstatic, but I knew they were not angry with me. Rain was probably wondering if she was dreaming. Alexander was without a doubt wondering how to tell this story at a later date. Alexander never seemed to lie because he never had to. He never did anything wrong and the only penalty for this was an extreme reluctance towards risk. Perhaps this is the attribute that Rain felt so attracted to, and, at the same time, deeply afraid of. Her father was a bishop, and though he loved his God and showed his love through prayer and sermon, he had never been able to fully show his love for her. It always made me wonder how it is to feel rejected from the one place that never rejects. To know that you are overlooked. Perhaps this is how Rain saw her Alexander. Perhaps this is what caused Alexander's simultaneous sufferance and jubilance when in her hands.

"At least this is better than calculus." Alexander said.

Rain did not speak, only watched our progression towards the door, holding Alexander's hand, as if in a dream that did not need her voice.

Because I was responsible for the circumstances that surrounded both my friends, I felt obligated to go first. Thus with one more wave to Dr. Chambers and Sammy, I hesitantly checked to make sure my incidental escorts were behind me and stepped out of the office.

Although the hall that lead to the waiting room had appeared outside the door, it vanished as soon as I stepped through it. We had stepped into a kitchen that seemed small at first, due to the mountains of Coke cans covering the floors. It seemed as though the cans had started in the garbage and slowly made its way throughout until whoever had been drinking them eventually gave up, turning the entire kitchen into a macrocosmic refuse.

"The home of a Coke addict." Alexander said.

He had managed, somehow, to make our bizarre situation into something infinitely lighter than it felt.

A soft ringing echoed off of the aluminum cans and a sign began to flash in the corner of the ceiling, which read "MAIL APPROACHING" in large red capitals. I assumed the cans were vibrating because of the noise—perhaps the tones had struck some kind of pitch with the metallic surfaces, like breaking glass with the right note. However, the cans rumbled more and more, and we realized that the sound was not affecting the cans at all, but rather a person that we had not seen beneath them. An electric guitar came first from amidst the cans, then the hand that held it, and eventually a head and upper body. His unkempt hair contrasted with his well-trimmed side-burns, as if trying to say that he deeply respected some things, and simply ignored everything else. His long nose spoke of Italy, which he vigorously rubbed with his hand, scratching an itch that would not go away. He stretched and groaned, keeping his eyes closed, as if rising from his bed with utmost reluctance, unwilling to let go of darkness.

Once his eyes were open, he surveyed us casually. The guitar hung on his body on a strap that went from shoulder to waist. While looking at an unknown piece of matter from his nose, he said "I've created a personal policy regarding hallucinations, due to their increasing presence in my life. I'm blaming the caffeine. Yesterday I woke up and I thought my father was cutting up my mother and placing her parts into a plastic garbage bag. Now I am apparently seeing three kids that look my age who are probably from New York City, judging by the girl's black pants and sophisticated glasses. Anyway, my policy is to humor all such visualizations and treat them as a means of further self-exploration."

"Do you mind if I smoke?" Asked Alexander.

"Not at all. There's an ashtray somewhere by the sink"

"I'll just use one of your cans, if you don't mind."

"Mi Casa Es Su Casa. I'm Constantine by the way, but I suppose you already know that, considering the fact that you are coming from my mind."

Perhaps it was Alexander's cigarette, dispersing trails of smoke and filling the room with its trademark smell that caused Constantine to question our existence. He had turned his guitar around and positioned it accordingly. His hands did not look like those of a dexterous and talented musician, but rather those of a man who loved music so desperately that he was willing to make do with whatever hands he had in order to play. He concentrated on the strings, occasionally looking at a point between our heads and the ground. He looked confused, as if trying to play a complicated chord or uncertain as to why we were there.

He was playing some kind of lullaby, using the rhythm of the flashing sign for his percussion. The three of us were anxious for answers. But Rain was the first to interrupt.

"What does that flashing light mean? Where are we? Why are all these Coke cans here?"

Constantine replied,

"Who are you? What are you doing in my house? How did you get in?"

Rain fell silent. We stood, awkwardly, until his lullaby ended and, with the impression of mercy, lightly touched Rain's shoulder.

As if this were no surprise, he responded

"The mail-woman is coming. You're in Southampton, New York. I became addicted to Caffeine the day I fell in love with her. I set the sign up to ring when she turns the corner so I never miss her."

I looked through the door we had stepped through and saw a study in the place of Dr. Chamber's office. Monitors and video equipment sat on shelves. There were videocassettes with dated labels and the occasional phrase for further detail, such as "DOG ATTACK #3" or "CRYING TWO DAYS BEFORE THANKSGIVING." Lights began to blink. The monitors turned on one at a time, until the moving image of a lady became the focus of the room. Close-ups, side views and aerial shots followed her towards his house. A sign below the largest screen displayed a meter that slowly decreased in value each time she took a step.

The numbers had reached double digits when I felt Rain's hand upon my shoulder.

"We're going. We're thinking this is your adventure, not ours, and since we've somehow warped to Long Island, both of us agree that we might as well take advantage of a free trip to Quogue with no traffic from the Long Island Expressway."

Mesmerized by the implications of Constantine's room, I responded with a nod.

"This is some pretty fucked up shit, Phaedrus. You're welcome to come with us if you want."

I knew there were at least a few moments before I had to make up my mind. I doubted Constantine would let them leave before the mail had been delivered. He had already joined me in the room, resting his guitar on its stand and sitting down in an oversized leather recliner that hid his entire body from view. Alexander had politely refrained from entering the room with his cigarette. He was standing over the table in the entryway, moving paper with his hands as casually as possible, in the way one carefully moves his fingers behind the mask of chance. Eyes inspect whatever has been touched, as if only from instinctive curiosity to know what one has touched by accident. His smoke continued its ascent from fingers to a cloud, like halos stacked upon each other.

Rain cautiously approached the Italian guitarist, arms crossed, chest sunken inwards to express fragility. She looked over his shoulder. Without lifting his head,

Constantine opened up—ever so slightly—to Rain. Perhaps it was her beauty, or the humility with which she had approached him. The extent of Constantine's devotion had begun to make Rain feel ashamed. Nothing in her life seemed noteworthy in comparison, for although there was no straightforward profit from his enterprise, the magnitude of his dedication made her efforts seem pathetic.

"Sometimes, falling in love means realizing the significance of certain things that previously seemed insignificant". he said, "Telephones are no longer convenient—they are divine connectors. Beds stop feeling full with the weight of your body. They become heavenly clouds of rest that only serve half their duty when someone else is absent. Mail is no longer junk—it's an oracle. It offers communion with the world and has the power to grant wishes. You go to the post-office and they don't let you tread on the temple's sacred ground. Instead, you give the mailman your offerings and your payment. The temple sends out missionaries, who deliver messages from various oracles. I fell in love with the mail-woman the first time she delivered my mail."

Rain tried to see what he was doing, but his privacy was absolute, and all she could study was the movements of his pen and the top of his head.

She replied, "And she doesn't love you?"

"I don't know. She hasn't responded yet."

"She ignores you?"

"She hasn't responded to my postcards."

"You send her postcards?"

"I send myself postcards."

I had drifted out through the hallway and into a gigantic living room. The roof was visible, supported by vast beams that formed triangles above me. There were antique chairs and sofas, adorned with lamps and other exotic artifacts. I walked over to Alexander, curious as to what he was looking at so secretively. It was a pile of postcards—thirty or forty at the very least—written with the same hand and stamped over with "return to sender" signs.

Rain was still attempting to understand Constantine, who was madly dashing his hands over the desk, inserting blank tapes and adjusting different instruments.

"So you're trying to win over the girl you're in love by sending yourself cards that she delivers."

"Yes exactly."

"Why not send her a card instead?"

"It's not that simple."

"Why not?"

"You're in the way of my zoom lens."

Rain adjusted her position so that Constantine could reach the contraption. The mail-woman's image became increasingly defined, filling more and more monitors. The room that had been so silent became immersed with sounds and colors.

When the postal woman put her hand into the mailbox, 3-D models started flowing over his computer screens, noting temperature, heart rate, galvanic skin responses and other such data regarding her hand.

"She's melancholy today. I think she gets melancholy when there aren't any clouds out."

"How do you know she's melancholy?"

Rain's hands were on her hips, apparently irritated on behalf of the mail-woman's privacy.

"I installed a sensor in the mailbox that's kind of like a really modern mood-ring. It can tell me how she's feeling to an incredibly precise degree."

Rain lost her temper. Alexander and I were used to it. Constantine, on the other hand, was not, and caffeine mixed with panic launched him from his seat. He was instantly behind Rain, who had started marching to the front door.

"Are you crazy?" Shouted Constantine, "You can't go out there! She's still here! You'll ruin everything!"

Rain was so full of steam her response was closer to a locomotive than her own voice.

"You're the crazy one! If that girl really is so virtuous, which she apparently is, she isn't responding to your cards because she doesn't read them. It's against the law! She isn't allowed to! It would be *invading your privacy*—a rule that you don't seem to grasp."

She had stopped—inches from the door—to focus on Constantine, who looked much shorter than Rain in that moment, although though he was taller in reality. He swallowed whatever response he had intended to use, only capable of mumbling something in resemblance to a question regarding Rain's intentions.

"What are YOU going to do, Constantine?"

I was the only one who could still see the monitors in the den. After the mail lady closed the box, she had started to look at the house and sigh.

"She's staring at the house and sighing heavily." I declared, eyes still on the screens. Rain shot her hand out and pointed at the door, like the pointing-finger-stamps on Constantine's cards..

The girl outside took an even deeper sigh, leaning into the palm of her hand so that there was just enough tilt to resemble a dreamer or a confused puppy or tired toddler or something of the sort. I narrated, saying "Okay, bigger sigh, tilting head, looking at sky. Wow, she is so obviously looking for attention. She should have a sign or something."

Constantine did not laugh, nor did Rain. Alexander might have, but he had been in the process of lighting another cigarette. Constantine's hands were cradling his head and he was shaking.

"You don't understand. It can't be this easy . . . I've built so much around it. *So much around it,* for nothing? The stakes are too high for me. It has become my excuse for committed fascination."

Rain was nowhere near sympathy. She crossed her arms and shifted her weight to the right hip.

"Why do people always build things up too much?"

The mail-woman was starting to back away, adjusting her grip on her canvas bag. She slowly bent down to tie her shoe.

"She doesn't want to leave but duty's calling. She's tying her shoe as slow as she can."

"You are so pathetic" Rain hissed, "how can you waste your intelligence, your talent like this? Go out there. Now!"

Constantine was looking at the floor. Alexander smoked his cigarette. Rain had the look on her face that Alexander and I loved watching from a safe distance. I knew how Constantine felt though. Every man encounters women who look so perfect he doesn't want to move because he fears the whole image might crumble. Kind of like a deer in head-lights, or if Medusa was beautiful. So ideal he gets guilty just thinking about her, for he thinks that if he had anything at all to do with her--even just being some guy who thinks about her--he would tarnish the perfection with banal, inferior identity.

Constantine confronts the mail lady: Go to chapter 505
Constantine does not confront the mail lady:
Go to chapter 112263

Chapter 505

Constantine lowered his right hand to the strap that held his guitar. He carefully unlocked its clasp and it fell onto the marble floor. He held the guitar out to Rain, who took it from him. After a heavy sigh—perhaps even heavier than the girl had sighed outside—he opened the door. Rain looked funny holding the guitar. His hand print slowly evaporated.

We ran into the den. Rain jumped into Constantine's chair. Alexander and I watched over her shoulder. There was a wide-screen shot of the front door and the mailbox, from which the girl had removed her arm the moment Constantine had opened the door. He squinted at the sun, holding his hand up to block the rays. He was still holding a can of Coke.

"You must be Constantine," she said to him. The visor of her blue baseball cap hung seductively over her eyes. Alexander was next to the stereo, which was amplifying their voice—there must have been a microphone in the mailbox. He turned up the volume.

Constantine was grinning apprehensively.

"That's me."

"He's so eloquent in person, almost as captivating as those cards," Alexander said without smiling. Rain and I could tell he was being sarcastic.

They continued to flirt. She was very good at flirting. She batted her eyes like the wings of a social butterfly, occasionally tilting her head so her hair could fall down and swing over her shoulder.

"Too much caffeine is a bad thing, you know." She was saying to Constantine.

"Oh this stuff? I know, I only do it occasionally."

"I hope he doesn't invite her in" Rain said.

"Our work here is done." Alexander said, putting out his cigarette.

Alexander started dialing his cell-phone and Rain stood up from her chair. They were going to call a cab. I continued watching the monitors. Constantine and the postwoman were hitting it off. Of course, Constantine had a considerable advantage, having studied her for an entire year. The girl had put her bag down and was leaning with her hand on the mailbox again. Constantine, trying to look laid back, had balanced the empty can on the arch of the mailbox in order to rest his hand beside her own. The sensors were registering everything on the mailbox—Constantine's hand and her own, along with the circle from the can. The hands were glowing red with heightened body heat. I watched the shifting colors of their palms. It made me think of satellite photography and weather forecasts on television.

"Don't you have to deliver the rest of the mail on your route?" Constantine asked her.

"Yes, but there's only one letter left today."

I quickly stood up, told Alexander I would see them soon, and ran out the door. I approached them with a generous smile and took Constanine's hand into my own.

"So nice of you to have us Constantine, but I had better go. Rain and Alexander called a cab. I'm going to walk for a little. Is there anything I can do before I leave? Take the garbage out? Clean the dishes? Your kitchen is a mess."

Five minutes later I was walking out of Constantine's driveway with a letter in my hand. It had been addressed to a house down the street.

Alexis was wearing large sunglasses and was sitting on a chair that hung on metal chains attached to the porch's ceiling. She was not swinging on it. It was not swinging at all. Perhaps the metal chains had rusted over. Instead of trailing back and forth in a way that might have shown a history of motion, the chair was still enough to make her cigarette smoke creep up towards the ceiling in a straight line. As straight as the chains attached to her chair.

She was smoking on the porch, using her elbow to support her smoking hand. The sight of her caused me to wonder how deadly things manage to seem elegant. Perhaps the smoke of cigarettes define the body of a smoker's secrets, because death is such a mystifying thing. If one could shoot himself in slow motion, and watch the bullet gradually tear through air and skin and tissue into vessels, step by step, there might be many more such suicides.

I approached the steps that lead up to her porch, carefully avoiding the cracks between the slabs of marble that made up her pathway. Her lawn looked perfect, as if even the ambitious weeds between the cracks had been placed there for a natural look.

"I have a letter for Mr. Morris. I'm doing a favor for the postal service. I have to make sure he receives it."

I expected her to pause, make everything seem more significant. However, she responded immediately.

"He's at work," she said, then slowly breathed more smoke in with her breathe. I couldn't tell if she was looking at me. The porch was her stage—I felt like a small audience. As if she had not gone back to her dressing room between performances because she felt more comfortable on stage. Sometimes it is very easy for people to get used to lights shining on them, rather than around them. When the operating light shines onto a patient, he knows that he is in his surgeon's hands. When we are illuminated for others to focus on us, we no longer have to concentrate on anything outside ourselves.

I raised the letter, balanced on the palm of my hand, between her eyes and mine.

"Could I leave it for him?"

The sun was not acting as it should have been, for although it was behind my right shoulder and was obviously shining on the porch, I had to squint when I looked up at her. I felt intimidated for some reason—as if under an interrogation lamp without being questioned. She looked over to her left side, observing the clouds, or the adjacent house, or something in her head that only she could see.

Exhaling, she replied.

"If you leave it here for him, I won't touch it."

"I see."

"What do you see?

She quickly—but by no means abruptly—returned her head in my direction. A fluid breeze caused me to look notice the trees in her yard. It did not make sense that they were palm trees—Constantine had said this was Long Island.

"There are palm trees in your back yard. I thought we were in Long Island."

"A gift for my father. Transported from the Florida Keys."

"He must have important friends."

She chose to pause at the strangest times—as if reading a script for the first time, testing a new environment on a planet she had grown accustomed to.

I walked up the porch steps. They did not creek or bend under my weight. They were not made of wood, but rather a strange looking material that looked like stylized fiberglass. Some ultra-modern design incorporating ergonomics and aesthetics. Upon stepping up to her level I noticed that the hanging seat was not hanging at all. Phone books, scrapbooks, bibles, and albums and flattened newspapers had been stacked beneath the seat, high enough so that the chains did nothing.

"What's with the seat?"

"Got tired of swinging back and forth. I'd rather have it still."

"I'm surprised."

Because she knew I had an explanation, there was no need for her to ask. She used her voice carefully, so that I hung off every word. Like reading dream sequences in profoundly symbolic literature, or subtle clues in mystery novels. I wanted to give her my whole spiel, but was uncertain as to whether I could fully explain things with the time I knew I had before she would lose interest, like an audience hearing the monologue of a character who is not yet intriguing.

I picked up a blue piece of chalk from the floor and drew the diagram at her feet.[9]

"The way I see it, the straight line is conformity. People fall into lives of repetition, so there are no surprises or extremes. The wavy line is most desirous—one must accept the lower positions in order to have the higher positions."

"You have to take the bad with the good." She added.

"Yes. But what people get confused about is which section of this course is good and which is bad. They think these are the good parts—"

With yellow chalk, I outlined the following

"—And these are the bad."

However, I believe it is this misconception that causes so much emotional chaos in the lives of those who exist outside conformity, for in actuality, these are the optimal areas, and these are the worst.

I put the chalk down and looked back at her. Feeling the need for some kind of conclusion, I tried to tie it all together.

"And if people could understand this, I think we would have a better grasp on our emotional positioning, and thus increase our ability to interact, cooperate, and combine forces."

She sighed and extinguished her cigarette by dropping it into a can of soda.

"So you're attempting to graph, or, like, analyze the mechanisms of the heart and mind with a sin wave function and whatever y equals in a linear context. How quaint. Why?"

"I know. It's ridiculous isn't it? But so many people are objective. So skeptical. I call them pessimists and they say they aren't pessimistic, just realistic. It kills me every time I hear that. People want to understand the illogical in a logical fashion. So that's what I'm trying to do."

"Fine. But why are you surprised my chair isn't swinging?"

---

[9] All of these illustrations are expanded on in Illustration 9a-d

"It just made me think of this diagram. Pendulous motion imitates waves. But your stillness is the straight line of conformity. You don't strike me as a conformist."

"But if the line is up here—" She grabbed a black piece of chalk between her toes.

"—Then I am always in the same state of optimal emotion."

I was ready for this; for it seemed everyone had this thought when I tried to explain.

"Because in order to comprehend the zenith of emotional well-being, you have to feel the depth of emotion's most abysmal points. One cannot fully appreciate the peak of a mountain unless they have swum down to the very bottom of the sea from which it emerged. That's why the journey upwards, from the very bottom to the top is so much more important than merely climbing a mountain and coming back down. One who starts and ends in these places never fully grasps their status in relation to the grand scheme of things. Perhaps you are missing my point."

The palm-trees whispered with their leaves as they had before. The coconuts looked disproportionately large, as if about to fall.

"As a lady of the stage, I prefer this straight line of yours, because the best kind of theater is the kind that singles out a certain point on this emotional scale of yours . . . because good theater is the kind that singles out certain points on the graph, over and over again, without having to move up or down, because theater is outside of time."

I tucked in my lips, trying to come up with a response, but realizing that she was right, or at least grasping her explanation to some extent, I switched subjects.

"I'm not surprised you're an actress—you've got that drama vibe around you."

"I hear that a lot."

She lit another cigarette and simultaneously opened the front and screen door. I assumed she had been smoking on the porch because of some rule, but she casually walked into her house as if it did not make a difference.

"I think there's some lemonade inside."

I stood up, letter still in hand, and followed her in. I was beginning to understand her method of communication. Her state of awareness allowed her to skip over the irrelevant things I said, assuming I would understand her.

Mentioning the lemonade to me was an invitation to her life: Off of the lawn, up to the porch that was her stage and now backstage. I expected tech men to be walking about with microphones and black clothes, carrying props and moving furniture. But the house was empty. There were large posters that must have been antiques—from the middle of the 20th century. Charlie Chaplin, the Marx brothers. An autographed picture of Buster Keaton hanging from a clock. She must have had all the windows open because the temperature was not different inside, nor the general atmosphere—as if we weren't inside at all, but rather standing outside with a few obstructive walls to block our views of the exterior.

I followed her into the kitchen, which seemed almost as bare as the hallway—had there been no posters to intrigue a passerby. White cupboard, white island, white brown knobs. Silver toaster. Metal oven. White glasses. She ashed in the sink and pushed a glass over the circular island. I put the letter in the middle of the table.

"It's really important that this letter gets to him."

"Of course it is."

"Can you make sure he gets it?"

"No. But I can make sure it doesn't go anywhere."

I wanted to ask about her refusal to go any straight distance for her father when I realized that it might be a bad idea. A banging from upstairs, followed by the wailing of a grown child came down over us, which stopped abruptly when the phone rang only once and we were back in silence.

"So . . . you're an actress?"

Lighting another cigarette, she nodded affirmatively and finally removed her sunglasses.

"Yes. I'm an actress, but when I'm out of work, I volunteer for a pharmaceutical company. They give me these pills and I tell them how they make me feel. Some of them are just placebos, I think, but I'm not really sure."

"Don't you think that's kind of dangerous?"

"Yes."

She walked out of the kitchen to the bottom of the stairway. Looking in the direction of the noise, she shouted, "HEY FLORENCE, QUIT THE BANGING WILL YA? WE HAVE A GUEST!"

She walked up the stairs and, feeling uninhibited, I followed her up into a large room with a table, where a girl who must have been Florence sat carving wooden sculptures. She had long black hair and dimples on her cheeks that did not belong there. She should have grown out of them; a beautiful baby, stuck in a lady who was still just a girl. Upon further inspection, I realized what she was carving—couples in wedding attire, the kind on top of wedding cakes. There were tall ones and thin ones, black ones and Asian ones. Alexis walked into the room and put her hands on the girl's shoulders. Looking over her work, the girl smiled up at her, and then at me.

"This is Florence, named after the city in which she was conceived. She's growing up, becoming an exaggerated form of who she was before."

"What does your dad do?"

"He's a lawyer for Philip Morris. Helped win that lawsuit. They hired a helicopter for him now, so he works in New York and then flies out here. There's a landing pad in the backyard."

Speaking of the devil, the loud, repetitive thud of a helicopter steadily grew louder over rustling palm trees. The three of us turned around and looked out the window, where a helicopter made out of transparent materials released a tall man in a black suit and turned its engine off. His briefcase looked heavy. He was slightly leaning over in order to keep it balanced. When he got to us, he closed the glass window that looked out onto the lawn and the sound of the helicopter faded in accordance with the closing door. I handed him the letter. He looked confused. The kind of man one sees from time to time in cigar shops or jewelry stores, unsure of what to buy, or if anything that could be bought could solve a particular problem. A young man wearing a mask of a decade—with wrinkles and thick lines across his forehead, as if he had been frowning from not anger but frustration from the conflict in his life.

Alexis had put her cigarette out. What could her father have said about Alexis' smoking? She paused and put her hands over her face.

"Oh, hold on, I think I'm feeling something from the pills."

He gave her a concerned look, causing the lines on his forehead to get bolder. Putting the briefcase down on the grass, he placed his hand on her shoulder and softly said "Isn't there another way you can make money between gigs?"

After replaced the sunglasses, she said, "I consider myself a connoisseur of emotions and my body. I'm the best one for the job, and I'm helping the world in the process."

"Couldn't you just give blood or something?"

"They wouldn't want my blood."

"I see."

"What do you see?"

"Why do you always say that?"

"Because no one ever really sees what someone is talking about, they just say that to switch topics or something. Boy these pills are strange, is it just me or does the sky resemble marmalade?"

Her father wanted to say something, but didn't. The smell of tobacco was her odorous aura, but by no means a repulsive one. As if incense was her perfume and the men she had been pondering before her father came home were somehow melding with the smoke, repositioning her mind and bringing her confusion out onto her face.

We walked into the kitchen, where Florence had moved into the dining room table, carving a tall black man in a tuxedo and a rather heavyset woman in a wedding dress. Her father set his brief case down. It made a thud, providing an implication of abundance and with this abundance an impression of power and responsibility. He looked at the letter I had given him and, deciding not to open it, took off his jacket and loosened his tie. He went to the bathroom and we listened to running water.

"My father—you can call him by his first name, Rye—he comes home from work perplexed all the time. He loves me, I know that, and he hates his job, but he keeps his job because he loves me, and the circle goes around and around."

She wanted another cigarette, but resisted the temptation because her father was home. We knew he wanted to tell her something, most likely regarding her smoking habit, which she clearly wasn't trying to hide. If this was the case though, he had no way of confronting her. Sure, smoking is awful—it kills. But if it really is so bad, why does Rye work for Philip Morris? How come he flies to the office every day and file paper and attend meetings concerning the seduction of the world? Alexis smoked, which meant he was succeeding in his job. To ask Alexis to give up the cigarette that rested in her hand would have been ridiculous. Her friends reacted in different ways. It's a free country man, like, your father's mad cool. Or: I can't believe you're the daughter of a hypocrite, why would someone try to make a profit off of health?

Alexis laughed it off. Rye had issues.

In the kitchen, Florence had almost finished carving the figures, applying the last details, like the bride's lacing and the man's bow tie. Rye picked up the newspaper and pretended to read it as he thought about hypocrisy. He wasn't reading anything in particular and if the newspaper had been transparent one would see that Rye was staring at his daughter.

Alexis herself appeared to be uncomfortable. Perhaps it was the pills, or her craving for a cigarette, or the synergy from both. She put her hands to her temples and started breathing heavily, the way a man does before he asks someone to marry her. I was trying not to get involved, choosing instead to look at Florence's handiwork. She had even carved the hands of the figures that held one another, and on another pair, the carving of their embrace seemed so well defined that one could see how tightly they were holding one another.

"Hey daddy-o, do you mind if I smoke in here?" I don't suspect she was desperate, for she had been chain-smoking before his arrival. Perhaps she was just curious about the way he would respond.

Rye put the newspaper down on the other side of the room. Even Florence put down her wooden figures to observe. Everyone seemed to know a moment like this would happen some day, but no one wanted to look apprehensive now that it was actually happening. Rye withdrew a packet of his own, but instead of cigarettes, he withdrew a large joint.

"There's so much to discuss," he said to us, "and it's obviously hard for me to admit that I'm a hypocrite. All of you should know though, that I've decided to do something about it."

Alexis gave me the look that said it was time for me to leave, so I stood up and headed towards the door.

Before I left, before Rye had lit the joint, and before the important conversation could begin without me, the nervous man asked "Where are you headed, young man?"

"I don't know, back from where I came, or maybe somewhere new."

"Perhaps we can help each other."

There was some shouting from Rye and the pilot—who was still wearing his helmet—came into the kitchen with a large sandwich in his hands. He had put a linen napkin in his collar so as not to get his tuxedo dirty. He was a gigantic man; a circle with muscles and a neck so wide that maybe he had no neck and his head was attached to his shoulders. Florence came over to my side and handed me one of her figures. It was a bride, with long black hair and a pale complexion.

"This is for you," she said, "Perhaps you will use it on *your* wedding cake some day."

I thanked her, then boarded the helicopter with the pilot. I waved goodbye to Alexis and Rye, who waved back, telling me to stay in touch.

I could see the land beneath us through the floor of the helicopter. There were cars and roads; one long beach swept along the Long Island sound. Soon we reached the city and landed on the top of a large apartment building. I jumped onto the ground, my clothes started blowing everywhere in the wind. It felt strange to have the spinning blades force me forward, away from the vehicle. Not exactly forward or downward, but away. The pilot took his helmet off and screamed over the helicopter engine.

"This is where Rye told me to take you, he says there's a woman on the ninth floor that you should meet. Tell her who sent you and that he got her letter."

He got back in the helicopter, took off, and faded in the distance. I noticed he had been eating his sandwich all along, and I still had the small carved figure that Florence had given me. I opened the fire escape door and walked downstairs until a sign on the wall said nine. There was only one door and it had been painted the same shade of gray as the rest of the stairway. It was the color of battleships. I hesitantly knocked on the door and waited apprehensively.

After muffled footsteps, the door opened by a butler. He looked suspiciously like the helicopter pilot—gigantic, and dressed in a tuxedo.

"May I help you?"

"Well I'm not so sure, this lawyer named Rye just gave me a ride in his chopper and told me to stop by."

"Just a moment, please."

He left with a distinct walk that seemed appropriate for a polite giant. As I waited, I imagined him trying to catch dreams like the Big Friendly Giant, and wondered how high he could jump. He returned and gestured for me to come in.

"I am Domino," he said, engulfing my hand with what might have been claws, "I take care of Lisa. She is very interested in seeing you."

I followed Domino through an elaborate apartment, decorated with antique furniture and paintings. One even looked like a Magritte—the one where there is a canvas in front of a window and the picture on the canvas is the background in the window. It was beautiful, and I paused for a moment to take in its beauty. The carpet was extremely soft. I had the urge to take off my shoes and dig my toes into the ground. Domino stopped when he saw me inspecting the picture and stood beside me.

"People have asked Lisa if they could sleep under this picture. Sometimes I think the story of the picture's owners and its experiences are even more interesting than the picture itself."[10]

"Can I touch it?"

"I would tell you absolutely not, but the truth is, I touch it myself every once in a while, to make sure it really is just paint."

I raised my hand and touched one of the clouds, eyes half closed, wanting to feel the texture that Magritte had mastered so well. I cannot say how they felt, but I hope whoever reads these pages is disappointed when I say they did not feel like clouds, for, of course, they were not clouds at all.

Domino walked into the living room and announced me to Lisa. She was sitting on a sofa, looking out the large window onto the city. There was a large grand piano in her room, extremely well polished. In pristine condition, no doubt.

"So," She said "You're the one Rye just called me about, Phaedrus Dumai. Tell me, don't you just love those wedding sculptures his daughter makes. She makes a lot of money

---

[10] When Domino said this, he was not referring to the Magritte, but the photograph hanging next to it. I failed to notice it the first time I went to Lisa's home because of my obsession with the Dutch artist. The photograph depicts an adolescent boy in some kind of museum. The picture looks completely normal until investigating the boy's expression, which cannot be deciphered without reading the title: *"Picture of the victim's son, taken by the victim moments before his attacker stabbed him to death."*

from specialty bakers. Rye didn't seem to know how you came into his life, but you certainly managed to change things in the course of an hour."

"I wish I could take responsibility, Lisa, but I really didn't do anything at all. I think I was just there at the right time. So if you think I make things happen, I would say you are wrong, I just seem to be in the right place at the right time."

Only once she had leaned back in her sofa did I notice the harlequin cigarette in her hands. She was watching me passively. The venetian blinds were tilted downwards just enough to hide the details of her face. Her long black dress, made of a reflective material that bent according to the light, revealed bare shoulders and sank down around her feet. Trails of smoke, not unlike the smoke that had surrounded Alexis, rose softly towards the ceiling. Smoke and light mixed together, illustrating the other's presence in a dance outside of gravity. A silver necklace wove around her, stopping seductively above her breasts. It was dancing with the light too—it was as if each and every part of her existence had some supporting role inside her ambiance, and the combination of these elements created a character that went beyond a simple person. It was the way she influenced her setting. There seemed to be an atmosphere about her, twisting in the smoke. How long had she been sitting on the couch, in such a strange apartment, smoking from that harlequin? I wanted her to continue, but she seemed expectant, somehow confident that I would talk first.

"That's a nice piano."

She did not reply. She nodded for me to sit. The smoke began to nudge me forward. I sat down on a red recliner.

"I hate pianos. No one knows why I hate them so much. Rich melodies, always grounds for good accompaniment, it is hard to find anyone around who really hates piano."

It felt like both her voice and smoke were talking harmoniously. She spoke as though she had practiced her line a thousand times, conversing with a mirror every day before she brushed her teeth. It had become such a ritual that by now, when the moment had finally arrived, she rattled her lines off with such ease there was a slight suspicion.

Domino entered the room and handed me a crystal glass with what appeared to be brandy. As he handed it to me, he whispered, "She just had her Valium before you arrived, so you could say her lips are kind of loose."

I was desperately curious as to why she hated piano, but did not dare ask. I had realized by then that if I was supposed to solve a problem or help with one, the dilemma would present itself to me. Only pessimists dig up problems that should otherwise be left alone.

Without any inquiry on my behalf, the whole explanation just came out of her, as if she had been dying to tell her story.

"It's really quite stupid, you know, I'm a little embarrassed about it, to tell you the truth. My father was an asshole.[11] He treated me like shit, and I hated him for it. He was fat, or should I say, immensely overweight, and he would eat large meals while sitting in the living room. He liked to eat and he liked to play that damn piano, and so to save the precious time he had, he would simply eat at the piano. Eat and play. Eat and play. I hated to watch him eat, and the worse thing was the maid, who had to constantly wipe the keys of that piano to remove the greasy residue his fingers left. I would cry in my room and listen to the random, off-key notes that the maid hit by accident as she cleaned. I hate pi-

---

[11] Lisa's father was indeed an asshole. His lust for money had eaten his heart away, and many of his acquaintances presume that his music was the only way he stayed alive so long. While attending his last year of business school, he had rented an apartment with four other students. Because of their stinginess, there were many discrepancies regarding the purchase of common household items. Because of this, there was never any toilet paper. Ironically, the four business students were compelled to use old editions of the Financial Times as a substitute. Many years later, one of his maids asked him for petty cash so she could restock the servant's quarters with toiletries. As he gave her the money, he replied "I'm a capitalist, but I'm not an asshole." And laughed uncontrollably through breakfast.

anos because I hate my father, for they are one and the same to me."

She stopped suddenly, as if she had been cut off in mid-sentence. She looked away from the piano, out the window into the trees outside.

Away from the piano and out the window.

After a few moments had passed, I replied, "Lisa your father is long dead and now the piano is yours. How can you let the past dominate your present life?"

She shrugged, walked over to the piano, and banged out a few bars of Rachmaninoff. Of course, I was amazed. She smiled and asked me if I wanted a drink, because she was going to have one and another valium.

I said, "No drink thanks, but if you might spare a valium, I would much appreciate it. My mind is in a blaze right now."

She withdrew her necklace, in such a manner as to seduce one with the elegance of pearls and ornate treasures. She unfolded the largest pearl, which had been hanging at the bottom, revealing a small, hollowed cove that held two pills. Pills within pearls.

"They found this pearl at the bottom of the sea. My father had its insides grounded out and mixed in with his ashes before we threw them back."

Go on to Part II

Chapter 666

I did not realize how intoxicating Bobby's drinks were until I found myself in the altered state they had produced. Certainly not like being drunk, but definitely some kind of parallel between the two. There was a spiritual feeling that came with it that alcohol could not induce. Perhaps if Jesus and Einstein had gotten drunk together, I would have felt the same way they did whenever they laughed at the same joke. It could have been the medicine that dangerously intelligent wizards took in order to stay sane. Bobby had brought it out of a room beneath the deck with a pair of crystal glasses, informing me that it was from a sacred village, somewhere on the fuzzy border between India and Africa. Its villagers used the stomachs of slumbering virgins as tables on which to sell and drink it, and measured it by the tears of crying shaman priests.

"What do you mean between Africa and Asia?"

"You don't think the ocean is a fuzzy barrier?"

"Good point."

"There are many places in the sea that have not lost their secrecy to charts or satellites. These people could never be understood . . . they play a game each year, during a certain festival I was lucky enough to see, which they called Pullomachessbull. They cover the horns of two bulls with flint on a cloudless night and watch them fight each other in the grand display of sparkling light that showered around the bulls whenever their horns clashed."

The sun had set, gradually giving way to fields of individual light. Someone told me once that humans were supposed to live in a horizontal fashion-as they did when the world was not so populated. The urban lifestyle is so chaotic because it forced us to live vertically, in skyscrapers that stand directly next to one another. In the beginning, life had been simple, for mankind stood alone with nature, oblivious to others of their kind. Minds of the most simplistic nature. Then we joined and with collective thought sought distant lands, moving from one place to another. If one stood on the ground, distant from these tribes, he would see a simple line from here to there; a perspective with only one dimension. Then we settled. There were villages and farms, territories and borders and suddenly, one could have looked down from the sky and seen us on the planes, as two dimensional beings. And as our society grew we expanded upwards into buildings and eventually skyscrapers, completing our ascent into the third dimension.

Bobby returned to the wheel of his ship, slowly approaching the edge of a small, hidden dock. There were loud voices and the sound of clinking glasses. Silhouettes and darkened figures could be seen through patches of foliage that had been positioned along the floor of the dock in order to conceal what lay behind it. It was hidden between two tall apartment buildings in such a way that it became completely camouflaged from the river. I never would have noticed it if a series of candles had not been placed along the sides. I thought of illuminated runways that airports use at night.

Bobby kept one hand on the wheel while throwing a rope to someone on the dock and began tying the ship to various pegs.[12] I could not tell what the person on the dock looked like. He seemed to blend in with the night. I hurried over and threw the remaining ropes to the person on the dock. After doing this, Bobby came to me, holding a black marker and a name-tag that said "DANTE" in typed letters.

"This is a costume party, but since you don't have a costume, so this will have to do."

He handed me the pen and pinned the tag to my shirt.

"And where is your costume?"

"I am the entertainment, I don't have to wear a costume. Come on, we're late."

We stepped onto the dock, and walked behind the foliage. I noticed that we had thrown the ropes to someone dressed in

---

[12] While Bobby was running around the boat on our way to the party, he had stopped for a moment and said "Sailing is all about 'nots . . .' How many *knots* are we going? Tie this *knot!* Do *not* put your head behind the skinner! All this sailing gives me *knots* in my muscles!"

a guerilla suit in a white waiter jacket. I followed Bobby through a corridor created by a series of tall hedges. The path ended in a square courtyard. We quickly walked to the center, where a large fountain poured water from a small circular plane onto larger and larger planes below. A stage had been constructed at the bottom, where Bobby began setting up.

He obviously did not need my help, so I looked around. I felt as though I was standing inside a cube. The right, left, and front walls were the sides of buildings, all equal in size, creating the courtyard within that held the party. A paneled glass ceiling hung above, the same size as the walls and ground. Everything was covered by ivy, making it hard to differentiate between each partition of the walls.

Guests were sitting at a bar along the left side of the wall, watching other guests or a television that hung down from above. It would have felt like a normal costume party had the guests not looked so much like their costumes. The fairies seemed to radiate bright light when they smiled and even float whenever they moved. I went to the bar in search of a drink for the two of us. The bar tender was dressed like Adolf Hitler. He looked just like him with the moustache and the uniform, the polished hair-cut parted to the side. However, his sleeves were rolled up and he smiled while pouring drinks for everyone. I sat on a stool and he approached, leaning over the counter, resting both hands on the edge.

"Drink for you?"

He even had the German accent.

"Two."

He poured two tumblers of the same drink Bobby and I had been drinking. He poured it through a fountain hose that must have been connected to a keg somewhere below the bar.

"Friend of the host?"

"I'm with the music."

"Friend of the music is a friend of the host."

He resembled the dictator so well that I wanted him to act cruelly. His kindness was a contradiction I had a hard time handling.

"Great costume." I said.

He didn't respond, only looked down at the floor, smiling as he poured a drink for someone else. I wanted to ask him if his face was part of the costume too, but noticed a large notebook next to my drink that the adjacent woman was writing in. There were elaborate diagrams, labeled with extensive notes and mathematical equations.[13] I sipped my drink, trying to get closer to the pages. I must have been too obvious though, because the pen stopped moving, causing me to inspect the hand that held it. It was Marilyn Monroe in a red sequined dress. Her hair was pulled back, and she was wearing glasses. Nevertheless, it was definitely her. Only then did I realize who the woman at the museum had been. It was Marilyn Monroe of course. I wondered how it was possible to have missed this when we had been in the museum.

"Excuse me, but you're blocking my light," she said to me.

If she wanted me to go, she would have to be more direct than that. I stepped back and moved to her other side, which made her smile and—thank God—put her pen down. Few men get the chance to sit with Marilyn Monroe, and though I know it couldn't really be happening, I indulged in the illusion.

"What are you writing?" I asked.

"Nothing really, just a few ideas I had about the universe."

She adjusted the frames of her glasses while inspecting whatever she had just written. I heard a few chords come from Bobby's direction, who must have been tuning up his instruments. She seemed to hear as well. Returning to the pages, she ran her hand through her blonde wave of hair and appeared to be thinking internally. I picked up the drinks, turned around and almost knocked Jesus over on my way

---

[13] See Illustration 9

back to Bobby. He wiped away the strands of hair that had been sticking to his face as soon as he dropped the large wooden cross that he had been carrying. I immediately tried to help him, but he abruptly turned his head and shouted, "Get out of the way asshole! Can't you see I'm trying to carry this thing?"

I wanted to apologize, but he was already up and on his way across the room. Before I could catch him to apologize, he was already gone. He had disappeared through some hidden opening in the right side wall. I shook it off as much as possible, then handed one of the drinks to Bobby on my way back to the bar. He had already started to play. I knew this wouldn't be a problem though, for if he could play all those instruments at the same time, then surely it would be possible to put his lips to a glass—if only for a short while.

Back at the bar, a young man dressed in Victorian clothes was leaning against the counter in the same place I had been sitting. He was looking up at the opposite wall, where a woman was standing on an ornate balcony. A beautiful girl in white lace stood on it, holding the edge so tightly that her knuckles could have almost pierced through the overlying skin. I would have kept on marveling beneath her beauty if she had not screamed down to the bar, her voice high pitched enough to make my ears reverberate.

"Why are you such a bastard Romeo? You act so immature!"

The young man, who must have been Romeo, did not even reply to her with words, only raised his fist towards her and displayed his middle finger, simultaneously drinking from a large glass, filled with the same strange drink that everyone was drinking.

"If I were you," replied the girl on the balcony, "I would go to hell, and stay there."

He did not respond at all. He just turned around to pay full attention to his drink, occasionally eyeing the soccer game that was on the television by the bar. I could not find an opportunity to speak to anyone—Marilyn Monroe had disappeared, the bar tender was working on the other side of the bar, and Romeo only paid attention to his drink and the game. With nothing else to do, I awkwardly watched the television until one of the teams scored a goal and everyone who had been watching the game began to jump and cheer.

"ALRIGHT!"

"Three cheers for assholes!"

"Assholes! Assholes! That's our time!"

"Go assholes! G-O-A-S-S-H-O-L-E-S!"

Bobby was fully devoted to his song by then. Nothing could have interrupted him. I did not understand why we were cheering for assholes. When the shouting calmed I touched Romeo's shoulder, hoping he would not react to me in the same way he had to the girl on the balcony.

He immediately turned around and looked at me, then moved his stare down to the empty surface of the bar so he could hear me better.

"Excuse me!" I shouted. He did not react, but in so doing, allowed me to continue speaking near his ear.

"Why are we rooting for assholes?"

He gave me a perplexed look, then put his head back in the same place I had whispered to him. After repeating myself, he smiled and then began to laugh. I did not know why he was laughing, but laughed with him anyway, figuring that I probably couldn't look any more stupid than I did already. He pointed to his mouth, meaning that he meant to talk to me. I bent down in the same way he had.

"Not assholes, ARSENALS! The English soccer team! The world cup is on and everyone here is rooting for the Arsenals . . . they still have a chance of winning!"

After saying this, he moved back so that his eyes could watch my own and witness my transition from confusion to coherence. They were audibly supporting their team, I realized, not a derogatory name.

Although I did feel somewhat foolish, I was relieved to find out that I had not done something worse. I had wondered if perhaps I had broken some terrible law or rule that no one had told me about before entering the party.[14]

But Romeo had forgotten my blunder before I even started blushing. The game was already over and the television channel had been switched. Basketball now—the Chicago Bulls were losing to an unknown team. Interest in the contents of the screen had dropped dramatically after the Arsenal's had secured their victory. Romeo appeared to be the only one concentrating on the game. He had lit a cigarette—eyes still on the game—and started conversing with Marilyn Monroe about her universal theorems.

"There's a connection with everything," he was saying to her, "The way a butterfly flutters over poppy fields in South America is related to guerilla warfare in Lebanon."

Marilyn Monroe was listening to him with intense amounts of concentration, making me feel rather jealous.

"Oh yeah," she added, trying to keep up with Romeo, "like precognition."

"Actually no, not at all. Precognition is just a window people use to try and understand it. Time is irrelevant, and the past, present, and future are happening simultaneously, so everything simply *is.* We try and explain these connections with terms like precognition and chance. Little do we know that the connections we see are an infinitesimally small fraction of the perpetually existent connections between all things that go unnoticed."

When Romeo realized that our looks of confusion were the only response he was going to get, he fervently inspected the bar for something to use as an example. The Bulls had managed to pull themselves together and were winning now

---

[14] I was once attending a review session prior to a final exam. Being the youngest one there, I had the least experience in preparing for such intensive trials, and had barely gathered the courage to ask some very basic questions about the course's concepts. Although the teacher's assistant responded to these questions politely, one senior member of the class had laughed in a condescending manner each time I spoke up.

After this had happened several times, the professor raised his voice. "Never criticize the questions that another person asks young man! Would you like to be judged by that which you do not know?"

by a single point. But the future looked grim for Chicago—with only three seconds left in the game, a foul had been called against them. The other team had missed the first foul shot, and thus only had the chance to tie and go to overtime. As the member of the other team prepared to shoot, Romeo whipped around and extended his cigarette out in front of Marilyn's face.

"Newton's law of gravity states that every object emits a force of attraction on another object, the strength of the force depending on the masses of each object and the distance between them. So even though the apple that fell on Newton's head was pulled to the ground by Earth's gravity, the Earth was also pulled a minuscule distance towards the apple. Now, the Bulls could lose if the other team scores this last foul point, but what they aren't counting on is the force of this cigarette as I drop it into the ashtray."

He held the cigarette over the ashtray and waited for the man to shoot. The ball went up into the air and Romeo released the cigarette, which ceased to be a cigarette as it fell towards the ashtray because the dimness of the bar made its burning ember the only thing visible. Like the fireflies I had seen by the Metropolitan—as if one was falling from grace in order to make the unseen forces of our universe visible for one ephemeral moment. And as this kamikaze firefly descended I could also see the basketball on television, flying towards the net.

But of course, the ball never even touched the rim—as if had suddenly gained weight and could no longer follow the naturally arced course that the player had marked out for it. It was a dead air ball. The Bulls had won. The three of us leaned over the ashtray, watching the last embers fade away.

"That," Marilyn said, "Was the cigarette that saved Chicago."

Go on to Book II

Chapter 6

I leaned back in the soft recliner, talking. The way he wrote in a pad from time to time made me feel important. I felt relief each time a part of the story came out.

"I suppose it seemed right to delay the situation with the strange lady and follow my father. But maybe I just chickened out . . . took the easy way. It was the proper thing to do, meeting my father's friend's and all. Explain my proper attire and introduce my father to the lady in red—a surefire way to appease him."

I paused for a second, taking a breath that felt like confession, then continued.

"So I handed her the peanut and left with my father, too afraid to look back."

Dr. Chambers had been my psychologist since I was eight. A good man. He reminded me of an ape when he crouched in his brown leather chair, causing his arms to look longer than his legs. Sometimes the sagging skin of his face, with drooping, bloodshot eyes reminded me of pit bulls. For the most part though, he was a wise old owl with thick spectacles, and that comfortable looking physique that older men who spent their years well carry with them. I celebrated his ability to dabble in parapsychology. We both agreed the only reason scientists were scientists was due to their fear of unanswerable questions.

I had caught him early in the morning—the perfect time to see a therapist. I was ready to bring up the subject, for it had been in my mind too long. I told him everything, from my drunken friends, to the lady, to the statue of Gnesh that only we could see, and on into my father's appearance.

"Well," Dr. Chambers replied, "I suppose we should take a look then, shan't we?"

I paused, then nodded reluctantly.

We both stood up and the office, full of old furniture, leather bound books, and cultured nick-knacks, silently regressed into their respective compartments. Everything in the room slowly regressed into appropriate compartments in the wall until we were standing in an empty room, like the space inside a cube. Dr. Chambers was the pioneer of such technology, and with his special instruments, we were able to create a replica of my memories, as well as surveillance recordings in a holographic environment. Our protocol consisted of observing my memories, then, secondly, the recordings of various surveillance cameras.

I approached the single white cord extruding from the wall and placed its cap over my head. The Doctor spoke commands to the computer, and the night I had been pondering came into focus. Many of the faces and details of the night were blurry, for I did not remember them. However, the woman was completely clear. We paused the holograms, so only the Doctor and I were moving. We stood next to the lady, just before she started talking to me.

Dr. Chambers and I strolled around the Temple a bit. He stroked his beard as doctors do sometimes, making casual remarks about the event, mentioning how blurry the guests were, wondering if it was because they were so boring, or perhaps it was only the drugs I had taken that night. He said it in a complimentary way though, as if agreeing with my priorities.

We made our way to the temple, passing through guests or objects that were in our way. Both of us were used to the concept of walking through holograms. Other than tripping over the wire occasionally, the only mistake we made was bumping into the walls of the real room, which we had a very hard time seeing. This was rather embarrassing, like running into a screen door. We would make witty mime jokes, then continue.

The statue of the Elephant was there, just as I recalled. We looked at it for a long time.

Returning to the lady and my silhouette (for there was no image of myself), we replayed the experience several times, discussing how I felt about each moment. Trying to understand why I felt so concerned about it. Both of us noticed how generic the lady seemed, how she failed to fit in for some reason.

We watched my father approach us, observed his repression of emotional expression. You could see it in the way he held himself so nervously, as if he might be judged at any time.

We had paused the re-enactment, so that the issue could be discussed, and I walked around my father slowly, trying to understand his grin. It was like a perfect fusion of benevolence and armor. Each wrinkle seemed a different recollection of our past to me, until the rivers of his folded skin ensnared my memory, causing the entire room to bend and shift, morphing through selective landscapes of my mind.

Accustomed to this kind of activity, the doctor calmly closed his eyes to keep from getting sick and gave the appropriate commands to the computer, simultaneously snapping me out of the trance and returning us to the empty white room.

"Perhaps we should watch the surveillance tapes now."

We had been through this a hundred times. I did not want to know what had really happened. I reluctantly removed the cap and sat down Indian style, absently gazing at the floor. I listened to Dr. Chambers call up the appropriate recordings in the museum's files, monotonously speaking to the system.

The file was finally accessed and my view of the white floor was replaced by the fountain's still water. Cautiously keeping my head bowed, so as not to take anything in before preparing myself, I stood up and walked along the water, enjoying the illusion of its presence. I began to look around. Just as I had effortlessly walked among them that night, I moved through the crowd, comparing faces with jewelry, handshakes with stares, and the different stances of each guest. I recognized many of them as friends of my family, whose images filled countless picture albums in my mother's library. People I had been recorded with through time by cameras and canvases, articles and rumors.

It felt to me like walking through an album in my mother's room.

But the doctor pulled me away from these thoughts and back to the matter at hand.

"There are some rather interesting difference between your memographic hologram sequences and the actual surveillance renderings."

The elephant, of course, was nowhere to be seen, and I noticed that the waiters were serving some kind of caviar. The sight of it began to make me feel nauseous—not only because I hated caviar, but also because it meant my fears were true—it was not as I remembered it. The window was almost as reflective as it had been, but transparent enough to see my friends on the other side, desperately trying to get my attention. Dr. Chambers took the program off pause and we observed my attempts to see them, and their frantic waving by the glass. I looked around for the lady in red to appear, but remarkably, she was nowhere to be found until she stepped out of the crowd to tap my shoulder, just as the waiter had disappeared. We played the tape over and over, but could not see where she had entered, or any evidence of her existence until the moment she appeared behind me.

"My God, she looks just like Marilyn Monroe," He said.

Of course, I thought, that is the face I could not place. How could I have missed it? I felt very stupid.

I made sure I was on the other side of the fountain when we walked over the bridge, so I could closely watch her hands, trying to find the pennies she had dropped into the fountain. However, they appeared to have been in her hand all along, even during our first confrontation by the wall. Pennies in one hand, champagne in the other, I had missed them entirely.

"We seem to have another paranormal event on our hands, Phaedrus, proven by the fact that this lady, who I will call Marilyn, cannot be traced until the penultimate moment of her self-imposed introduction. We cannot assume that she is one of your hallucinations, because your father also sees her."

"And my friends can see her too" I said, replaying the tape to show them outside, swaying their hips suggestively.

"So the only difference is the elephant, and the caviar."

I walked over to where the elephant should have been, wishing for some evidence of its existence. We turned the system off, adjusting ourselves at first to the blank room, then to the antiquated furniture that slowly moved back into place.

Sitting back in our seats, we pressed onwards with our discussion until my time was up. I stepped into the waiting room, thinking of the errands that my mother considered imperative. The room was usually only occupied by the secretary, who would silently type at her keyboard and speak in hushed, whispered tones, to patients like myself. I was surprised this time though, to find three friends of mine occupying the room. Alexander and Rain sat casually on a couch, talking in circles as usual, while Antonia gazed blindly at the pages of a magazine. As love has many cycles within cycles, so did the games they played with each other. They were beautiful to watch. hey were always caught up in their circle games, unable to see the ultimate simplicity that they created together.

They were my age, both with attractive features that, on anyone else, would have been labeled as faults. Rain had ash blonde hair and pale, white skin. But upon the manipulative flesh of bones and body, its tone of white became cherubic, as if she was the daughter of a priest.

She fitted well, somehow, with Alexander's talent of story telling. His father had been an actor. He was a connoisseur of music too—so skilled at matching an occasion with the perfect song it made one think of wine experts, matching vintages and dates with recipes and menus. These qualities made Alexander a DJ of conversation, particularly where humor was concerned, and so the two would bask within the tangents of their dialogues. The reaction that Rain had were perfectly in harmony with Alexander, and so they both became entranced with the other, as art will sometimes control an artist, due to its innate desire to exist.

Alexander spun his stories, like a DJ mixing records, watching Rain react like dancers on a hardwood floor, searching for the right turn of the table. Catching rhythms, surprising her with higher frequencies until laughter and interest soared high above the grounds of common conversation, causing her angelic skin to glow and her ash blonde hair to bounce in resonance.

Rain would do the same to Alexander, creating the effect that mirrors have on one another. She would date other men, returning to him now and then, raising his heart back up while she refueled her own whenever it had been emptied on the freeways of obsession and control.

And then there was Antonia, sitting in a single chair, enraptured by her magazine. She was the most attractive girl I had ever seen. High cheekbones. Shining eyes, dark skin. A small, compact body. She was exotic, in that I could not tell where she appeared to be from. A different place entirely.

As Rain and Alexander were caught within their private symphony of circles, Antonia seemed trapped to the one her magazine created. Still in the first two years of high school, the allure of conformity was still strong and, due to her overwhelming beauty, she did not have to look much deeper for comfort or guidance. Some may say the beautiful live easier lives, but no one ever sees the disadvantage of a person's beauty. The beautiful are envied. The beautiful are never seen as anything but beautiful, and are never examined for the things that make us who we really are. To so many people, Antonia was no more enticing than her magazine. Her head was bowed over the glossy pages flying past her eyes, as flip-books mimic tiny worlds.

I said hello and all of them reacted with a quick turn of their heads and shining smiles. I was surprised to see them there. I knew Alexander didn't believe in therapy, and neither did Rain. As far as Antonia was concerned, it could have been anything, just like me. I was still surprised to see her though, in the room I always waited in before entering my mind.

I inquired as to what they were doing that night, for it was a Friday night, and everyone is looking for a plan on Friday night.

"Honestly, I don't know" said Alexander, and Rain nodded her head in agreement.

"My sister and I are throwing a party at my house. Usual crowd, usual thing," Antonia said, who had already returned to the glossy pages.

I could not take my eyes off of her legs, the totality of their seduction. The perfect strand of hair that fell down from the confines of her ponytail. I could go with Antonia, chase her all night through the tall thin Brownstone that her parents lived in, competing with the other desirous men.

The thought was both intriguing and repulsive, but so was the potential for a night with Rain and Alexander. I would play a role I was comfortable with by then—that of the third wheel. I admit that I was rather good at it, like playing Mercutio, entertaining the lovers, spicing up the dish. I could have it either way—chase love through the circles of conformity, or chase it through circles that my friends had built around each other.

Plans With Antonia: Go to chapter 64
Plans With Rain and Alexander: Go to chapter 3

Chapter 3

There was definitely some kind of relationship going on between Sammy and Antonia. I knew it, because Sammy was slouching in her arms, eyes rolling upwards, meagerly holding the bloody razor he must have slit his wrists with. Making my way to Rain and Alexander, Sammy had burst through the door and fallen into Antonia's arms. No one knew how to react, so we all just stood there in silence for a moment, listening to Sammy ramble. We were very surprised of course, but for some reason it was not the fact that he was dying in his lover's arms that I was pondering, but that he was supposed to be in Sweden, where he lived.

Antonia finally screamed at the receptionist to dial 911. An ambulance was on the way. Convinced of an impending death, he started talking to Antonia in hushed tones, like lovers sitting through an opera. He told her that he knew about Dr. Chambers' technological advances—that his presence there was necessary. The reason why, he said, was because he had discovered a serum that made one incapable of falsely describing himself. However, the recipient had to sincerely want the operation, regardless of what a subject thought he wanted. Because of this, he had been unable to prove it worked, and had kept the discovery secret until finding a way to want it. Only before dying could people ever want the power to truly define themselves.

I could not help but notice the elegance of Sammy's blood as it fell onto Antonia's olive hued legs. As if there was nothing macabre about the situation, and if I had been Sammy, I would have enjoyed the drama. Not afraid at all.

I ran into the doctor's office, surprised to find the room back in its empty state. The corded helmet rested in Dr. Chamber's hands. He urged my assistance in connecting Sammy, as if he'd been expecting him.

I have never run down those halls so fast, throwing Sammy's arms over my shoulder in one smooth motion and rushing him into the office. The nurse was screaming in regards to the way he would lose even more blood if I held him like that, but I felt instinctively that the more time he spent away from the office, the more we would lose in the long run.

In some sick combination of relay race and emergency room, Dr. Chambers connected Sammy as soon as his head came through the door. Rain and Alexander came into the office to assist, not realizing that the doors locked automatically. Dr. Chambers didn't notice them, fervently fumbling from voice commands to keyboard strokes. Finally, the meager details of the room gave way, and Sammy's session started.

Rain and Alexander, who apparently hadn't known anything at all about the analytical engines of the office, watched in amazement as a standing image of Sammy appeared over the one that I had carried in. He was not bleeding, and looked as though nothing had happened. His thick-framed glasses were no longer there, and he wore a pair of white pajamas in place of his black pants and vintage leather jacket. He looked at Dr. Chambers with child-like eyes, then at the ground somewhere between himself and the doctor.

A picture slowly emerged where he was staring. As these images came into view, we all seemed to forget that the real Sammy was lying on the floor, either dead or close to it.

There appeared to be an empty room at first, then chairs, a desk, posters—as if watching someone move into a room in fast motion. A man was sitting in front of his computer at his desk. When I looked into the monitor's reflection, I saw that it was a younger Dr. Chambers. More hair. Less wrinkles. His eyes were less baggy and he sat with a better posture.

All of us, including the other Sammy, moved into position so that we could watch over the young doctor's shoulder. He was silently checking his email with nothing but the clicking of his mouse and the occasional shrug of his shoulders in reaction to various data displayed on the computer. He leaned back suddenly, as if his interest had grown so much it actually took up space between the screen and his own face.

The angelic Sammy said, "You were in graduate school. Your old friend from Princeton, Ashta, sent you an email, containing a link to a certain web-site. He said that he had made the first step in crossing the bridge between mind and technology."

"Whereas I had been planning on building the first brick of that bridge. I didn't think it was there . . ."

Dr. Chambers mumbled,

" . . . Ashta took a step on that bridge. He knew it was already there. This is where the two of you had disagreed. Unfortunately, Ashta had to die take that first step, and so do I, in order to keep the progression balanced."

The young Dr. Chambers looked into the screen as the web-site loaded and eventually became complete. There were diagrams of circles and lines, displaying Ashta's process.[15] There was a note, addressed to Dr. Chambers:

Bill-

We both discussed Camus' statement that no man has ever dared to truly describe himself. Perhaps this is why we are still working on the bridges between mind and technology, art and science. However, once someone has achieved a state in which he is capable of truly knowing himself--of understanding each small particle that makes up his entire essence--he will come to an understanding that time and space do not exist. I have found this way. I have followed this path because I believe it is there. I know that you do not believe that such a bridge already exists--that you are going to have to build it. I think this is true, in a way. I'm taking the step from the creative side of this bridge. The side on which our minds are based. One day you will take the step from the other side. The side of logic and technology. Let me ex-

---

[15] See Illustration 1

plain. The universe has built its bridges in a way that keeps the world from crossing them until it is ready. Imagine a seesaw, each end touching two separate sides. If one were to step on one side only, it would tip, negating the intended transition. Thus, two steps must be taken at the same time, one from each side, towards the middle. We, together, will take these first steps. As for the next steps towards the center, I must leave them to the future you will one day know as the present. I already died for the first step.

See you around,

Ashta

We watched Dr. Chambers anxiously access the next link and wait. Everyone grew anxious, except for Sammy of course, who seemed sufficiently prepared. The room was empty again, and though I felt extremely nervous, it was nothing compared to Dr. Chamber's apprehension. He had begun to sweat profusely as soon as the image of his former self had faded away.

The stillness was longer than it should have been. Everyone stood around, waiting for something to happen, wondering if anything should be said. The dramatic impact of silence can only last so long before it begins to look amateur. I looked at Sammy's dying body as it took its final breaths and began to wonder if perhaps we were waiting for him to die. With this thought it mind, his breathing stopped and something resembling a tunnel as large as the room appeared behind Sammy. After a moment of inspection, I recognized the tunnel to be composed of blown up images of the young Dr. chamber's monitors—displaying each other in the same way two mirrors that face one another reflect into infinity. A massive brown object—apparently the enlarged image of Dr. Chamber's head—occasionally blocked the tunnel that the monitors were forming.

Sammy spoke.

"When we know ourselves completely, time and space become irrelevant, and everything exists as one. That is why I had to take my life. Ashta and I are the first step, and by means of our ascent to this plain of awareness, you, Dr. Chambers, were able to get the data you needed to build a machine that could recreate the contents of a person's mind. Thus, I am taking the step from technology's side, while Ashta took the step from the side of his mind."

Dr. Chambers was shaking his head in amazement. He franticly opened his hands to Sammy with a look of resignation.

"Yes, I saw this tunnel—with my head and everything—but I thought I was just hallucinating. Then, after this tunnel appeared, data starting flowing into my computer and my mind together, providing a way to build this equipment."

"So you have seen us as we truly are: Sammy continued, "I know you still do not believe it. I wonder if you'll ever realize it at all. Regardless, we are all a part of the next steps towards the fulcrum of our universe's perfectly balanced bridge."

He looked at me, then at Rain and Alexander. His tilted eyebrows formed a stare that screamed enticement and adventure.

"You did not come here by accident."

I had been able to deny everything until that moment, but Bobby had spoken, and afterwards, I could lie no longer.

"So I guess that's where I come in . . . with the next step. That lady at the party told me I couldn't avoid it. That's why we could see her, even though she wasn't really there—affecting me without touching me. This all has to do with that night at the museum, doesn't it?"

"Yes. Although Dr. Chambers would rather look at it in terms of a scientific anomaly, others like you, Ashta, and myself see it in purer form. These perspectives may seem different now, but as the steps are taken, the differences will fade away, like images within these walls, until they are finally one. Our simultaneous evolution of universal consciousness and technology reflects this. All opposites are slowly coming back together—to the same place. Opposites exist in order for something to know itself.

"In the future, we will all come together, completing the bridge we're starting right now. But the most wonderful thing of all is that once we come together and stand on the fulcrum of this bridge, we will no longer have to stay in one place. We will be capable of joining any two points in our sphere of existence, and then experience these points simply by moving off the fulcrum in synchronized paces—maintaining the balance of nature."

"But what if the balance is accidentally lost?" Alexander asked, suddenly joining the group, "wouldn't all of existence be thrown into chaos?"

Sammy listened to this question and closed his eyes downwards, towards Alexander. Nursery school teachers, answering questions of existential toddlers.

"I do not know. Remember though, that everything happens for a reason, and although such a thing could only happen theoretically—due to the self-balancing system of our universe—all things evolve by expanding on the opportunities provided by spontaneous events."

Alexander backed away, for his only question had been answered. He had nothing else to say. Sammy stepped towards me and delicately touched my shoulder. Although I could not feel its weight, I could have told someone that it was there without seeing it. If one could feel light, rather than see it, that is how Sammy's hand felt. He looked at me, and because I was nowhere near as sure of myself as I knew he was, I did not have the strength to make eye contact. Instead, I rested my gaze upon his hand, contemplating its sensation.

"It's time for you to go now, Phaedrus. You can come with me, or you can stay here, and wait for another opportunity. The great thing about the gift you've been given is that you'll never stop getting chances. If you stay here, I can tell you that it would be for good reason. There is someone who needs your help, I'm sure of that. If you come with me, the universe will help him, of that, I am also sure."

"But who will help him?"

Sammy smiled "The universe, Gnesh, Love incarnate, the mail . . . everyone, basically. I suppose it's a win win situation for you, but I can tell you now that you are one of the key components in the next step, and eventually, you will have to face this fact."

Dr. Chambers was anxiously inspecting the tunnel's image. He was not in a position at that moment to advise me. Rain and Alexander were standing beside each other, no longer embracing, because, it seemed, they were no longer afraid. Alexander, one of my closest friends in the world, was telling me with the expression on his face that it would be unwise to let anyone influence my decision. I looked back at Sammy, he pivoted and opened his right arm towards the tunnel, then his left towards the door, which gave an audible click to notify us that it had been unlocked.

Tunnel*: *Go to chapter 3.14

Door: Go to chapter 100

Chapter 0

If anyone had asked me to describe a heart before the night of my departure, I would have conjured up the image of a bloody, mangled fist. A fist that had been smashed into a concrete wall to the extent that one could not make out one finger from another. The adventure began before I even realized that something else had ended. Through the experiences disclosed within these pages, I feel that I have learned the secrets of infinity. I would tell you them right now, but it would take too long. As every secret is unique to he who keeps it, no two people can exist within a common universe. Thus, it is impossible to share the cosmos—like passing water from my cupped hands to your own.

The right wall of the Metropolitan Museum Of Art in New York City is made of inward tilting glass. Adolescent boys and girls who were more or less the same age as myself would loiter there whenever we encountered weekend nights without decisive plans. High school kids would lean there, smoking pot that came from hidden labs beneath the streets of Harlem and drinking beer that had been bought with fake I.D.'s. It was just another place to go, and, by chance, I lived across the street. I would look out of my bedroom window and wait for a sufficient gust of wind to move the branches of a tree that partially blocked my view. I would look to see if anyone I knew was there, then try and convince myself to socialize. More often than not, I'd choose to stay inside and play with my computer.

The night I left my former life was a Friday. Bored with the artificial intelligence of overplayed video games, I went to the side of the museum. A few minutes later I was leaning against the wall with a group of kids like me, ambivalently waiting for something to happen. Deep down, I sensed that all of us were wishing for some phenomenal occurrence. But perhaps I was the only one who consciously desired such change, and the ignorance my peers had always hidden behind prevented them from coming with me. My mind had been wandering while resting on the glass—imagining what hearts might look like. The other kids had been singing monotonously, so that my body fell into a trance, unable to escape until they sang their final verse:

Take it down, pass it around, no more bottles of beer on the wall.

My mind had made it clear to me by then that it had had enough. I stood up from the sloping wall of windows and stormed towards Fifth Avenue, ignoring them each time they shouted after me.

Everyone was tipsy from the pot and booze. I remember heading straight towards 5th Avenue, but it must have been more like the jagged, erratic stride of a drunkard, where one tries to find the right place for his feet each time he steps, trying to make the turning world stay still. Only once did I look back. I saw them against the glass, in front of the illuminated room on the other side. It was gigantic, built specifically to hold The Temple of Dendur, an Ancient Egyptian building. Surrounded by water and light, it managed to look just as magnificent on the other side of its transparent wall as it did from within. The lights from inside shined through the glass, exposing the swaggering silhouettes of my friends so clearly that their shadows seemed overly dramatic, turning them into hideous, repulsive caricatures. The trees around me swayed without direction, submissive to the nighttime wind. Fireflies conveyed a thousand Morse-code messages inside the emptiness between each structure.

My corduroys itched and the restlessness of separation from my bygone flock was making me perspire. I passed the pay phone on the corner, fruitlessly attempting to come up with someone I could call. The museum looked massive as I approached the front of it, stretching to the center of the street, where it blended in with every other distant feature, losing its distinction and grandeur.

Although the doors had closed much earlier to public visitors, its fountains were still flowing and streams of limousines were lining up beside the entrance. A long red carpet had been placed over the stone steps, connecting the cars to the entryway. From a distance, the royal red carpet on the stone gray steps caused the museum to resemble a present, wrapped in splendid ribbon. A full moon hung over Fifth Avenue, with intermittent clouds that made the sky seem even more attractive.

I was walking towards the entrance but I don't know why. Guards with hidden radios were dressed in three piece suits, looking for suspicious things. Nevertheless, I had no problem passing them—as if I did not exist at all. The waterfall grew louder. Streams of thick white froth created the illusion of another wall. But like the shouts and hollers from my friends, the sound eventually faded.

I took the steps two at a time, with no consideration of the formal suits and dresses wrapped around the different guests. I moved through the doors, unnoticed. The lobby was filled with light so radiant that everything inside appeared to meld with the nighttime ambience, which every guest was carrying in—as if such impressions could be carried effortlessly—one only had to swing their nocturne mood over their shoulder and move on. Musicians played classical pieces on their instruments. Waiters served champagne on silver platters.

If I had had something to say to any of the guests inside I would have smiled appropriately and spoken, but in my semi-transient state I held no thoughts of speech. I strangely moved through the crowd, wondering how I could possibly move without the need to dodge or step. The guests fell into place, revealing a path into the next room. Instead of looking at the parting people, my eyes were fixed intently on the walls and ceiling. The decoration (tall, marble columns!) echoed sounds of conversation so gracefully I almost thought the people around me were genuine. For the first time, I almost managed to forget their lies. I realized then that the mark of true artists is their ability to show the beauty in that which first seems ugly. The museum had accomplished this, creating the illusion of sincerity in every guest around me, and none of them would ever know that they themselves were the greatest piece of art the Metropolitan possessed.

I felt a wonderful sensation—like the excitement felt while waiting for a sold-out show to start.

The party was being held on the other side of the glass wall, in the room that held the Temple Of Dendur. I felt inclined to look into the tilting windows, to see if the others were still there. I worried they might ruin things though. Perhaps they would try to follow me, or call attention to my presence. Slowly, I approached the glass, keeping my distance in hopes that I might see them first. I had a strong desire to confirm their presence. I wanted to make sure that I was in the real world, no matter how estranged I felt.

I could not see them—the lights inside and the hour of night caused the reflection of the banquet to be the only thing visible. I attempted to adjust my line of vision, hoping to find the angle that would make the wall transparent. As I tried to contort my body to see into the other side, a nearby voice caused me to jump in surprise.

"Aren't windows just for proving answers we find in reflections?"

It was a woman in a red dress, gracefully holding a glass of champagne in her left hand. I recognized her deeply, like I had known her face for my entire life, yet could not place the name. She had a disturbing face—each feature seemed too generic for an actual person. She appeared somehow, to have come from an entirely different world. A world that consisted of photographs and reproductions, where the way a person looked in one specific moment—as models in a photograph—was the only thing that mattered. As if she had been hastily pulled from a popular magazine and randomly applied to some unsuitable soul that, until then, had wondered aimlessly without quickening or slowing. Abruptly forced from its perpetual motion, confined to the contradicting features that stood before me. In a different circumstance, it is possible that many would have envied her.

I did not know how to reply, so I said nothing at all. I returned my attention to the crowd. Through the corner of my eye, I saw her looking in the same direction.

Eventually, she went on.

"You want to know what brought you here. You do not understand how you could be in such a place."

She said this without looking at me, but when I made a face behind her back (the kind of face I make when something sounds completely random or illogical) she instantly responded. She let out a short laugh, causing the straps of her Vogue dress to rise with those Cosmopolitan shoulders and Harper's Bizarre Arms. Before I could react to my frustration and confusion, a waiter came between us with a silver platter. I tried to wave the man away and yet she interjected, somehow managing to calm me down by resting her hand on my chest.

"I think" she paused, presenting the waiter's silver platter, "You should have a peanut."

There were simple peanuts on the platter, skewered with sandwich toothpicks. Although it seemed cheap on the museum's part, I thought nothing more of it. She took one from the middle of the dish and so I did the same, briefly noticing the silver plate's reflection of my face.

The waiter walked into the crowd and vanished. I was about to eat the peanut, but her expression of astonishment caused me to stop. I wondered if perhaps I had broken some taboo regarding tabloid lifestyles. Coming out of my existence which had been completely lacking in significance, the thought that each of my decisions mattered—regardless of their individual relevance—made me feel estranged. With a patronizing voice, she said

"No, silly. That's not for you."

By then my confusion had become frustration and I fired back at her.

"I'm sorry but what in God's name are you talking about?"

I said this very curtly, as if to say that, though the whole experience had been very intriguing, I was ready to get down to the point. She nodded, sipped the last of her champagne, and got down to the point.

"Straightforward. Doesn't like to beat around the bush. Excellent. It's often hard to show things to your kind because it is not possible for you to see it all at once. It seems to be man's instinctive nature to learn things indirectly, consequentially avoiding a direct solution. I am a manifestation of the artifact this benefit is being held for. I—the lady standing before you—have been created as a means of introduction and to let you make the decision of whether or not you wish to participate."

"Participate in what?"

I should have asked her something more specific, like who she was and what the hell this had to do with a peanut.

"In its benevolent assistance, allowing you to cut some corners—or remove them, I suppose—on the path towards enlightenment." She grinned rather enigmatically, then abruptly regained her serious expression.

"I don't understand."

"Of course you don't, which is why I approached you indirectly. You asked for the truth though, and I am here to provide it. I could tell you everything right now, but it wouldn't do any good. True understanding can only come through experience and repetition."

She walked away, towards the bridge that crossed over the moat of water that surrounded the temple. A handful of pennies tumbled out of her hand as she crossed, falling to the bottom. I do not remember her dress having pockets. Figuring it best to do whatever she did, I dropped my unused quarters into the water. It had always been my habit to avoid change where I could, for I disliked the way it weighed my pockets down. I always took advantage of fountains and wells, figuring that it could do no harm to throw spare change towards a wish. I no longer had anything in my pockets save a deck of playing cards. I had left my wallet and keys at home.

A portion of empty space had been roped off with velvet cords and silver posts in the center of the temple. The lady rose her chest in a boastful manner, like a general commanding his squadron. A toddler dressed as a cowboy. She pointed at nothing and spoke.

"This is Ganesha. The elephant God of India. Remover of obstacles. I am only one of its reflections, created to facilitate your process."

After she said this, my father, Kyo, stepped out from behind her (he is a short man) and said, "What elephant? This benefit is hosting the arrival of the cherished Buddhist rug, as you see at your feet. It's a wonderful surprise to have you here, Phaedrus. But don't you think you're a little underdressed for the occasion? And who is your friend?"

I was confused by my father's surprise appearance, telling the strange woman that she was wrong, and then this intangible tension around us. I had to laugh, and because I could not hold a serious expression, they smiled as well.

My father spoke the same way he looked—with a slight accent of distinction; aged. Somewhat foreign, his gray hair and wrinkles accentuating the image.

I looked down. There was indeed a beautiful carpet, obviously old, and a plaque noting its historical facts. There was some silence that neither the lady nor myself felt uncomfortable in, but it obviously disturbed my father. The lady and I looked up from the carpet at the same time, and right before my eyes, in the emptiness she had pointed at, the object had magically appeared.

It was on a pedestal, like any other artifact in the museum, yet seemed so radiant, so beautiful, one might think a pedestal unnecessary—that it could float on its own and be seen without any of the shining lights. It was an elephant with several hands, surrounded by a shining arch of bronze.

My father continued to look at the carpet, apparently unaware of the statue. With his head still bowed, he whispered "Beautiful, isn't it? We are fortunate it even got here in one piece. The poor thing had to take a million detours,[16] and yet miraculously arrived a day ahead of schedule."

---

[16] Perhaps the most significant obstacle encountered while attempting to transport this rug from its location was the location itself. It was kept on the peaks of a tall mountain. Its altitude would not have been a problem had it not been for the penultimate turn on the small, corkscrew road that lead up to the temple. The turn is very sharp, and the view around the

The lady and I were looking at the sculpture, yet I managed to murmur affirmatively. Even when my father was staring at me again, I could not look away from that which he was blind to.

"There are some people on the board of trustees you should meet, although I hate to think what they'll say about your attire!" He exerted a polite noise that must have been laughter and dashed off towards the lobby. My eyes could have stayed on the statue forever, but the lady was holding the peanut under the elephant's trunk between her fingers, looking at me. I rolled the toothpick in my hand, watching it spin around. I looked up to where my father had been standing. Somewhere in the calm but endless waves of boring people, Kyo was searching for his colleagues. I knew that he would find them. He would think of some joke to excuse my unusual presence. And the party would continue.

Just like that.

But then, there was this lady, offering something. I watched in astonishment as She lowered her hand near my own and the trunk began to move. There were whirring and clicking sounds. Gears that sounded ancient. I kept on switching my sight between the elephant and my father, who had no doubt found someone that I did not want to talk to. He was walking towards us across the water.

She said "Come now, or come later, either way, it's going to be a thrilling ride. It's only a question of how long you avoid it."

The winding noise inside the statue was growing louder. I thought that everyone would look in our direction. I realized though, that they were as deaf as they were blind to the statue's majestic presence. I pondered the way she had said those last words. It had struck an irritating chord in me, as if I had no choice in the matter. I felt a strong desire to rebel, I wanted to know that I could do whatever I wanted.

---

bend apparently so beautiful that an unwarned traveler will go right off the edge, crashing on the rocks below.

I saw my father, smiling. He would not hug me, only smile and say hello. Introduce me to the guests, no doubt, and make that joke about my clothes. There was the whirling sound within the statue, and a vacuous feeling near my hand, which seemed to be coming from the trunk.

Peanut ***Go to chapter 20***
Father ***Go to chapter 6***

Chapter 342

But apparently my words were not enough to make Antonia abandon her romantic fears of separation. The thunder struck in harmony with one great flash of lightning, and for one short instant I perceived that single drop of rain the deity had prophesied. It bounced off her umbrella and fell onto the ground below.

"You're going to catch a cold." she said, looking at the ground again.

"I'd rather catch a cold than let fear catch me. I have to go. Good luck with Sammy. Tell him I said hi."

I said this without moving, so she would be the first to leave. She sighed heavily again, then turned her body towards sixty ninth street, moving off into the rain, sheltering as much of her body as she could with the inadequate umbrella. I watched her melancholy strides, knowing she would not look back, but hoping all the same. Raindrops ran their courses down the pathways of my scalp and shoulders so that by the time I could not see her anymore I was completely soaked.

I thought about going home. I lived right across the street. It would have been simple to take the night off of me with my soaking clothes. I was sure the drinkers had left the side of the Met to find shelter somewhere and finish their booze. I looked up and down the street, trying to decide, watching the rain displayed on the pavement. If I had been anywhere close to dry, I would have felt obligated to get out of the rain quickly, but because I was so wet I couldn't care less. I walked down Fifth Avenue as slowly as one would if it was sunny

A limousine passed by, headed towards the museum. I assumed it held another guest, so was surprised to see it stop a few meters in front of me. I could not see into the tinted windows as it passed. I gave up and looked back towards the Met, which I had decided to pass one more time. I wondered if my father was still inside, flirting over drinks and conversation. Had he succumbed to his sweet tooth?

The sound of an automatic window tore me from these thoughts. I looked back towards the limousine and realized that the sunroof was opening. A steady rhythm from the music within grew louder and louder, until I recognized the beat of dance music—the transcendental nature of new-age club sounds. A combination of angelic voices and placating melodies, moving the rhythm of a dancer's heart towards an increasingly personal relationship with the music.

And just before the music progressed to an even more hypnotic state, two hands emerged from the sunroof, followed by arms supporting a head, then shoulders and eventually an entire upper torso. It was a young wolf with a head of scruffy black hair. Although it was night there were sunglasses over his eyes that looked like tinted squash goggles. There was a glowing green necklace around his head—the kind kids wear to raves and clubs. I momentarily assumed his appearance to be insignificant, but by means of another look in his direction I suddenly recognized his face. My mind exclaimed his name as he screamed mine, opening his arms as I opened my eyes and ran towards the car. It was Antonia's lover, Sammy Aldo, who should have been in Sweden.

"Simon! What are you doing here? I thought you went back to Sweden!"

"And what are YOU doing in New York Phaedrus? I thought you were going somewhere!"

"Going where?"

"Crazy man! Absolutely crazy! I thought you would have lost your mind by now you fucking nut!"

We both broke out in laughter. Two girls and another boy came out next to him, appearing just as jubilant as Simon did. Although I did not know one of the girls, I recognized the one holding Sammy. Her name was Coral Forest. They had met each other at the same party that I had met Sammy at two years ago. Sammy had apparently forgotten Antonia, turning to the embrace that Coral had been offering since the night they met. Although I did not know the other girl, I felt as though I recognized her from somewhere. Like I had kept a picture of her from a magazine over my desk for inspiration and encouragement—the kind of girl I dream about when those familiar thoughts of perfect love flow through my solitary soul.

I was certain that the other boy was Kirk, one of Sammy's close friends. He was a tall kid who had never seen a single episode of Star Trek. We liked to call him Captain.

"Well don't just stand there man, get in! We're taking you to the Tunnel!"

I suppose the pause I took before getting into the limousine was only for dramatic impact, used as a device for getting them even more excited about our unexpected encounter. I was certain their appearance was not accidental, just like the discussion I had held with Antonia—just as my father had predicted. Time or space would never again hinder the speed of my spiritual progression. One experience after another, lacking hesitation or confusion, as catalysts for self-discovery and outward understanding. The Met, Antonia, and now a night with Sammy and his company of friends. Their door hung open and out came Coral, grabbing my hand, pulling me into the car as the driver started moving again.

The light inside the car had been replaced by black lights, causing everything to glow. My eyes adjusted, causing feelings of sharp displacement whenever I looked into the normal world outside the window. A screen obscured the driver, so that we moved like passengers on trains, unaware of our conductor.

The girl I did not recognize was stunning in my favorite way—unique, off beat. Beauty that would have been ugly without some special, indescribable twist. The language of beauty became apparent to me, simply by looking at her face—a language shared only by DNA, completely foreign to the conscious mind. The girl looked over at Sammy and spoke something that I couldn't understand.

To my surprise, Sammy responded in the same language, and I realized everyone had turned to look at me. I began sweating nervously, making the leather seat feel closer to me, as if passing the border between comfort and restriction. Corral saw my discomfort and smiled before speaking to me.

"Lana is from Sweden—a family friend of Sammy's. Her English isn't hot, but Sammy knows Swedish of course. Which leaves Sammy and I to our own devices. It kind of sucks, but I feel worse for her, not knowing English and all."

Sammy picked up as soon as Corral stopped speaking.

"Lana says she recognizes you Phaedrus, but can't remember where from."

I looked at her profile as Sammy translated her thoughts, then studied the rotation of her neck as she turned back to my stare. I shrugged my shoulders and opened my palms, as if to say I did not know. Something moved within her eyes, and I took it as a sign that she had understood my gesture. I took out my cards. Sammy laughed and said something to Lana. I suppose he had informed her of my craft, and how I had told him on all too many occasions that like all of the most elemental things in the universe, magic was understood by everyone.

Or perhaps he had merely told her to act surprised, no matter how obvious my performance was, so as not to disappoint me. I fanned the cards before her and my knees began to tremble as they usually did. I had practiced those miracles so many times that they had become built up to something infinitely more significant within my mind than was the case.

I did not have to ask her to select a card, for everyone who has ever held a deck of cards has seen a bit of magic to accompany the enigmatic ambiance cards always seem to hold. Everyone knows how to select a card; I did not need to ask. She showed the card to my audience, then returned it to me, watching me shuffle and cut. Shuffle and cut. Focused on my hands. The sound of cards cascading and the animation that occurs by streams of various values and faces.

And the miracles began, according to my plan, for the benefit of all my spectators. I reproduced her card and then transformed it to another. My practice had paid off to the extent that I no longer had to watch my hands, and could watch the spectators instead. The greatest destination of a wizard does not lie within the mastery of his props, but rather within the mastery of his audience. He evolves to the point where expressions, reactions and emotions become the most important prop of all. It was this second sorcery that I became aware of in that car. Perhaps it was the depth of Lana's stare that made me think this, for never had I seen a pair of eyes so demonstrative of the owner's mind. I felt as though I had been performing for a clock all my life until that night, when I finally had a chance to do my act before its gears and watch the impact of my motions.

Lana noticed that I was not paying attention to the cards—that I was really going through the routine so I could study her face without being rude. She took her eyes off the cards and looked back in my direction. But Sammy, Coral and Kirk were still under the power of my cards, and continued to watch my sleight of hand while Lana and I spoke silently by means of the expressions on our face.

But eventually I had no more tricks to show and I forced myself away from Lana's eyes as the three of them slowly emerged from the spell. I looked over towards Sammy, who's eyes continued resting on my cards, and asked him to tell Lana that if bumblebees were absolutely beautiful, and could take the shape of perfect women, then perhaps they would resemble her.

He mumbled this to her in Swedish. Coral had stretched her body against him, resting her head on his shoulder, oblivious to Kirk, who sat adjacent to them. Once he had finished speaking, I looked back to see what she would do. I had hoped that she might smile, but instead she leaned away from me, saying something to Sammy.

"She says bees sting."

"Only when they have too."

Sammy replied for me and the car stopped suddenly, causing everyone to fall onto the floor. Ordered pairs and individuals had been sitting properly until the brake, at which point we found ourselves in a pile of limbs, like a game of twister in three dimensions. All of us were roaring with laughter, oblivious of how close we had come to serious injury. We did not hear the driver's footsteps as he came to let us out, and so Sammy fell out of the car, onto the dirty New York pavement, followed by cascading Coral and stumbling Captain Kirk. The driver, a large fat man who seemed to be pushing the seams of his tuxedo to their greatest level of tolerance, engulfed Sammy's arms with his massive bodice and brought him to an upright position.

I offered my hand to Lana, but she would not stop laughing in the corner. She did not even try to rearrange her tufts of disordered hair that blocked her view. I admit it had been a rather humorous moment, but had it been so comical as to warrant such laughter? She was laughing so hard that if someone had passed by us at that moment he would not have been able to tell if she was laughing or crying. She reminded me of me—the way in which Antonia had made me laugh so hard that all my confusion had fallen from my shuddering stomach.

Eventually she calmed down and I handed her the purse that I had retrieved from the floor during her hysterics. She took it and followed me out of the car, then nervously jumped onto Sammy's shoulder and whispered into his ear while looking at me. Sammy reluctantly transferred his attention to Lana and Coral slowed down in order to walk between Kirk and myself. She wrapped her arms into our own and tilted her head back.

"Lana has to stick with Sammy tonight, because she can't talk to anyone else. Sammy wants to be with me. I want to be with Sammy."

"And Kirk and I want to be with Lana." I said

Anxious ravers stood in a line between a chain of velvet ropes. There were cell-phones and pagers. Versace suits and Prada pants. Latex boots and colored wigs. Muscles. Sunglasses in the night. Handfuls of people would occasionally exit the club from the door on the left, dragging their sunken bodies into the street, searching for cabs or public transportation, sweating and frowning as if they had gone into the club and paid to have their aspirations confiscated and replaced with total despair. As they left, others entered, keeping the club at its maximum occupancy. A factory, dense with materials to forge and mold. Sammy and Lana ignored the entrance line and directly approached the center door, which was guarded by a black tied demon that faintly resembled human form. He wore sunglasses and his bald head reflected the disco lights from inside. Most would not consider the door behind him, for he appeared to be a wall, but Sammy and Lana treated him as though he were the only entrance, and the line of desperate sex and spandex was not even there. She gave me a look before reaching him, as if beckoning me. As if to say she was a wizard as well—she could pass through walls and conquer giants.

This is exactly what she did. She did not speak to him, only approached and stared for a while, letting Sammy do the talking. At first he only looked at her. Then the sunglasses came off. Then a smile. A laugh, echoed by Lana, who was just as good at working with reactions as myself. Finally, he stepped aside for us, and even touched my shoulder with his claw, as if showing his most secret side of innocence and sympathy. I could not help but make eye contact with him, just before he put his shades back on.

"My name is Domino."

"Phaedrus, nice to meet you."

"Nice to meet you."

He seemed eager to say more, but must have known that once I entered, I would no longer be able to hear him. There was a long tunnel leading downward, with red walls and carpet, reminding me of a mouth. It was hard to imagine what lied on the other side—as though the tunnel didn't belong in a club, but in a mansion somewhere in Greenwich Connecticut or the South of France. Kirk, Coral, and Sammy ran ahead, disappearing behind a turn in the tunnel. Sammy looked over his shoulder, right beneath a giant chandelier and shouted "Take care of her for a bit will you?" And was gone before I could respond.

So down we went, through the mouth-shaped tunnel and into the bowels of the discotheque. The neon colors that had looked so insipid outside had turned into a visible bridge between music and dancer. Make-up to intensify a woman's beauty. Secret dance of the highlighter pens, avenging the students who mercilessly used them. We scanned the dance floor and its contents, knowing that our mutual acquaintances had allowed the rhythmic jungle to absorb them. The DJ worked his turntables in a glass box hanging over the dancers on cables attached to the ceiling. With a momentum nearly too slow to notice, the box moved back and forth in the manner of pendulums.

I could havc stared forever. Lana must have felt the same way, because she urgently pulled me away and lead me into a separate room, where the lights weren't as bright or intrusive and the music was background noise instead of dominant mantras. Shapeless couches that were closer to oversized pillows. Square tables, circular tables, triangular tables, rectangular tables. Metallic tubing traced the ceiling, sucking tobacco smoke into its openings.

She chose the bar and we sat at stools with revolving seats. Before the bar-tender had mixed a White Russian on the house for her, Lana innocently tested the seat's range of motion. I held her shoulder and spun her around. Peasants spinning prayer scrolls on their way past a temple. The seat stopped and she took a sip from her drink. I admired her pursed lips, placed so carefully around the thin red straw that glowed under the black lights.

Lana was fishing around in her purse when Coral ran up to me, panting heavily. The light from the moving lasers and black lights reflected on her clothes, creating patterns I would have liked to focus on, but changed too quickly for my eye.

"That music is hypnotic. Sammy and Kirk aren't even in this dimension, I couldn't pull them off the floor."

"I think that's why they call it trance" I said sarcastically. Lana was still looking for something in her purse. Coral stopped smiling.

"What's wrong?" I asked her.

"I don't know, just a strange night. First Sammy's preoccupied with Lana because of the language barrier, now it's the music, and even though we've been together all night--"

"He feels far away. I think you've just proven that physical distance is irrelevant to love."

She slanted her eyes a little, as if suspicious that I was up to something--tricking her into being happy perhaps.

"Write about it."

"I will."

"I want my name to be Coral Forrest."

"You got it."

She went back to the dance floor and Lana removed a black box from the purse, which she unfolded to reveal a small keyboard. She typed with her index fingers, then pressed a button. A monotone, computerized voice emanated from the gadget.

"DID YOU MEAN WHAT YOU SAID ABOUT THE BEE?"

The soulless voice, combined with the expression on her face, was perhaps the most intense juxtaposition I had ever encountered. I nodded affirmatively. She typed again, and the distinct voice returned.

"BEES STING"

Imagine being doomed to falling in love with a drive-through operator and having no other way of talking except through the intercom she worked with all day. I typed, "ONLY WHEN NECESSARY. THEY ONLY STING ONCE. THEN THEY DIE."

She pushed a different button and read the translation on the screen instead of listening to it. I would have preferred to read her response as well, but I was too late, and out came the voice, like listening to a void.

"LIKE NUCLEAR WARFARE?"

I paused then nodded again. A moment of pontification, then I typed "WHY DIDN'T YOU USE THIS THING BEFORE?"

"SO IMPERSONAL. WOULD RATHER BE SILENT."

I wondered if all my nodding was beginning to get repetitive. She kept on typing.

"LIKE EMAILING A PERSON IN FRONT OF YOU."

I didn't want to nod again, so I typed "HUGGING IN MORSE CODE."

"MORSE?"

"NEVER MIND."

"LANGUAGE SUCH A BARRIER."

"KNOW HOW YOU FEEL. CAN YOU BELIEVE I PREFER THIS TO TALKING SOMETIMES?"

"???"

"KIND OF. I'M A WRITER. SHY. TYPE MORE THAN I TALK."

"LISTEN MORE THAN YOU SPEAK?"

"EXACTLY."

"ME TOO."

"CAN YOU STOP MAKING IT SPEAK? PREFER TO READ."

"OF COURSE."

Kirk came back with Coral. Lana discreetly hid the translator by turning around to face them and leaning backwards.

"What's up dude?" Kirk asked.

"I'm talking with Lana."

Coral laughed and Kirk gave me a wise-guy expression, nudging my ribs.

"Oh I get it. Universal language, right? Dialect of silent phrases?"

"Exactly . . . where's Sammy?"

She nodded towards the dance floor. I normally wouldn't have paid so much attention to her nod, but the whole experience with Lana had got me thinking about nods and gestures, and all such gesticulations we take for granted. Everyone looked in the direction of her nod and we were shocked to see the glass DJ cube swinging much more than it had been when we entered. It dawned on me that this was because the DJ had been replaced by someone else. Then it dawned on me that Sammy was the new DJ, and then the realization that Kirk and Coral had come back because Sammy was on his own again dawned on me as well. All this dawning made me want to yawn, yet I did not want to seem impolite.

"How did Sammy get up there?"

Without anyone taking their eyes off of Sammy, Kirk replied "You have to climb up the ventilation tubes and get the other DJ inside to swing over I think. That way the switch is mutual."

"No, I mean, how come they're letting Sammy DJ?"

I was asking because I had no idea what the political world of DJs was like. Did they fight for dominance or territory, like the primitive mammals whose instincts they extracted from those who danced to their music? Surely this is the effect such music has on dancers. It made me think of a girl I had met once in Florence who had fled to Europe in search of refuge from her clubbing existence in Capetown, South Africa. She told me once that the greatest DJs she had heard were able to connect with the core of their dancers, and would tease them like a well trained concubine with incomplete thrusts of melodies and rhythms until they were on the verge of exploding. Then they would release them into ecstasy by means of completing and building the music. She would talk about these things over bottles of red in the back of Italian restaurants when we were the last ones there, like an ex-member of some cult, recalling her incredible experience.

Everyone seemed very impressed by Sammy's mixing—even Coral, although I knew how much she wanted to replace his records with her body. Lana stood up and walked towards the dance floor. She looked over her shoulder as she had outside. Kirk, having missed no aspect of this silent invitation, looked at me while I watched her.

"What the hell are you waiting for?"

I stared at them. A boxer staring at his coaches before he enters the first round. They didn't have to say anything else—their presence was all I needed. I finished my virgin screwdriver and rushed to catch up.

Sammy had somehow thought to raise his head away from the turntables for a second and saw us coming. He ended the track and started a new one. It sounded like angels greeting one another in single harmonious voices. We walked into the pit of movement, as if we were the only ones there. We moved with the beat that had reached our ears beneath the angels, who had ended their greetings and started ardently conversing. And because we were moving with the music, we were able to reach the center of the dance floor without being pushed or shoved.

For the sake of recording my adventure as precisely as possible, I will let you know that I am a good dancer. So was Lana. I learned to dance in karate class, for martial arts teaches the most important lesson about moving—every part of the body moves. Every limb and every bone plays out its part according to the whole. Nothing is irrelevant.

Although I had danced to countless songs, with countless people, in countless places, I had never danced with anyone so closely. I mean this in the most literal way—I sweat a great deal when I dance because I move so much, so I always keep my distance. But this time it did not matter. She did not seem to care. We were happy, and when I saw Kirk and Coral climbing into the box with Sammy, I was sure that our entire company was finally content.

This moment of perfection, of course, is when Domino interrupted is. The bestial figure, wrapped in a suit that wasn't really a suit. It was more like a way to hide the scales, or tails, or fur, or whatever he held himself together with.

I felt disturbed by the fact that something always seemed to interrupt my happiness, and that nothing happened soon enough when I was sad. I wanted Domino to go away, to leave Lana and I to the music Sammy was controlling from the box above and let the night play itself out like one of his records.

But he was incredibly polite. I realized he even had a slight British accent to accompany his manners. He positioned his mouth perfectly by my ear, so that he didn't need to shout above the noise. He informed me that Mr. P (the boss, apparently) had invited me to a private function in the special section. Unfortunately, only I had been invited. My friends would have to wait. Of course, he would see to it that they were given extra special service while I was gone. I found it rather humorous to hear such a monstrous person talk so gently. He was like that big blue beast from X-men who always wore glasses and read books while hanging upside down. Goliath, making me an offer I could . . . accept or . . . refuse. We were still dancing with everyone else. Domino, however, stood in the middle of the circular dance floor, motionless, just like he had outside, like some focal point that every surrounding entity was anchored to.

I looked up through the glass floor of the cube. Kirk had taken over the tables. He was wearing gigantic headphones so large his head seemed dwarfish--as if Dumbo had become a DJ. His eyes were shut as they usually were when he dealt with music. The depth of his connection to the neo-symphonies he orchestrated brought a tranquil wave through his composure. Like Sidhartha and Ray Charles combined into the newest kind of art-form's artist.

Sammy and Coral were deeply embracing, whispering in one another's mouths and slowly moving to Kirk's melodies. Lana had taken a step away from me, returning to the dance. I took it as a way of saying that she would be content whether I stayed or went with Domino. She was ready for me to come back to her, or she could easily dance alone.

I followed Domino through the crowd and we stepped onto a raised terrace of booths and tables that must have been the VIP section. In the last booth there was one small man and one small woman. He looked like a cured Stephen Hawking with tinted glasses, wearing a black jacket over a turtleneck. She was an Asian woman with blonde hair, who watched the dancers apathetically, as if she had been looking at them for so long they were no longer interesting. Like natives of Paris beside the Eiffel tower.

He was eating an olive off the plastic sword of his cocktail glass, apparently unaffected by the cigarette smoke that she was resting under his chin. Smoke rose around his face like a halo someone had rotated ninety degrees as some kind of mystical prank.

Domino stopped at the table and withdrew a ring of keys. The woman brought the cigarette to her mouth, and the man bent forward to sip his drink. In this way, a keyhole the man had been blocking with his head appeared, and Domino slid the key into place, turned the lock and replaced the key just in time for the man to replace his head. The woman returned the cigarette under his chin.

The wall next to the booth revealed a hidden doorway, which Domino jovially ushered me through. He closed it behind us. I felt momentarily estranged by the normal light that had abruptly replaced the black lights within the club. There was almost no room at all in there, and I nearly panicked at the thought that I had just been pushed into a closet with a very large man. My eyes adjusted however, and I realized that there was a spiral staircase, almost too narrow, leading several flights up. There was a polished wooden globe at the end of the banister reflecting the light. Domino would have surely offered to lead the way if there had been room for him to get by, but the passageway was too confined. He could only manage to bow slightly, extending his arm upwards and point up towards the top. This made me laugh, because his elegant pointing made him look like some horribly ugly diva. A massive hunchback dressed in designer attire resembling Mike Tyson in drag. Domino laughed too, although I am not sure he understood.

"So sorry about the squeeze, it *does* get more spacious upstairs, I promise."

The staircase we started climbing was so narrow that our ascent felt like turning around and around on a rotating stair-master. I had no idea how he managed to fit up the stairs, and the fact that he wasn't making any noise made it even stranger.

"Do you have a day job?" I asked, trying to break the ice.

"I'm a butler."

I wasn't quite sure how to respond to that, and was thus relieved when we reached a wooden door.

"Just go on through, it's open."

I turned the knob and pushed with no luck.

"Other way, we have to step back a little."

We both reversed appropriately and I had to reach up this time to open the door. I thought I might have to ask Domino for a boost, but managed to open it on my own. I looked over my shoulder at Domino, who was grinning, eyes still hidden by sunglasses.

"You should see what a pain it is bringing women up here. They can't stand it. Of course, they never want to leave once they make it to the top."

I smiled and wanted to say something witty, but couldn't think fast enough and it was too late. The music from the party downstairs had slowly faded, and was suddenly replaced by the sound of live, genuine music and talking voices. Inside everyone was holding a drink and had eyeglasses on with thick black rims--the same kind geeks are defined by. However, there were many attractive, sophisticated people there, and some of them appeared to be wearing the frames without lenses at all. When I looked back at Domino his shades had been replaced and he offered me a pair as well. I put them on and was glad to find my vision untarnished.

We entered a huge room that could have been a penthouse apartment or a deluxe hotel suite. Balloons had been tied to lamps and occasionally drifted along the ceiling, having become untied and set free. The wall was curved and covered by large windows that revealed the Manhattan skyline.

Some kind of wonderful music was coming from the live band in the corner, which consisted of only two people, although it sounded like five or six. The lead singer had puffy black hair and the same silly glasses on. He was burning the place up. There was a saxophone hanging on his back while he played an electric guitar at his waste. When he turned around I saw a clarinet hanging from his belt, and every now and then he'd walk over to a small ragtime piano and bang out a few bars from that. He was singing some blues song about a girl named Penelope but I could barely make out the words and the drummer's whip-lashing hair and sparkling eyes took my mind off the lyrics. The guy was playing so many instruments he looked like a musical mercenary—as if Rambo had taken to nightclubs and was doing gigs in Manhattan with a new haircut and glasses. He looked like Buddy Holly, only shorter and selfless, as if approaching music with a saint's humility.

The song came to an end, everyone clapped while the singer caught his breath and wiped his forehead. His eyes soared around the room, like a comet, searching for someone or trying to find a place to rest. And this consideration of the comets encouraged me to look out the window, where the broad expanse of buildings stood illuminated outside. I could not figure out why so many lights were on at such an hour, but it seemed as though every window was lit from within. Shooting stars were no longer independent entities in space, but actually a civil society of wandering wishes that rested and recuperated in the vertical fields before me.

Tripods holding telescopes stood at the windows, set to varying heights and positions. Several guests were crowding around them, holding glasses of champagne and taking turns with the eyepieces. I was hoping that the music might start up again, but when I investigated their whereabouts I discovered an empty stage. The instruments which had been strapped over his body were carefully placed on the piano

I was avoiding the telescopes because they seemed so enticing—like saving dessert for last. In the corner of my eye I watched guests look into them and slowly walk along the walls. Signs that were too far away for me to read had been attached next to each. I knew that they were the main attraction--quite possibly the reason for the whole party. With my eyes fixed on the skyline, I strolled all the way down to the beginning of the room.

TELESCOPE #1
JUST A GLASS OF WATER

The future of Rain and Sammy Aldo

I looked at the singer, who must have been Bobby Snaplett, wondering what his story was. However, I suppressed the urge to look through the lens. I wanted to read all the signs first. Domino stood by the second, polishing the tripod's metal legs. He nodded his head in recognition when I stepped up to the sign.

TELESCOPE #2
TODAY AND TOMORROW
A retrospective

I smiled and went on without stopping.

TELESCOPE #3
TWO LOVERS
One sleeping, one awake

TELESCOPE #4
PENELOPE EVE
Subject of considerable remorse for Bobby Snaplett, tonight's guest musician.

TELESCOPE #5
ISIT AND ITIS
The twin brother and sister of a genie

Telescope #1 Go to chapter 29
Telescope #2 Go to chapter 5
Telescope #3 Go to chapter 11
Telescope #4 ***Go to chapter 601***
Telescope #5 Go to chapter 609

Chapter 20

I looked back at the peanuts in our hands beneath the elephant's trunk. I felt her body approach mine; the warmth of her hand as she put her lips by my ears.

"Let go," she whispered.

The peanut moved from open hand into the trunk, and the statue began to whir and click with increasing volume. The rings and crowns that decorated it slowly started to rotate, like gears of antiquated clocks.

I saw that my father was slowing down, along with everything else in the world. He smiled more as he approached me, as one would expect he might. I smiled back, then returned to my inspection of the statue, whose dials were spinning faster. The lady's grip grew stronger on my shoulder and she suddenly embraced me, placing her head in my arms as if looking for emotional support. When the dials appeared to be slowing down, I assumed the whole thing was stopping, but was shocked to find that the dials were not slowing down at all—rather, it was the world that had begun to turn around us. Looking at the spinning room began to make me dizzy. I realized why she had put her head into my arms.

Looking at anything else but the statue would have caused me to fall, so I held the lady tightly and concentrated on the elephant. It began to shine from within, and the sounds of the room were replaced with harmonious ringing. It sounded as though many church bells had been tuned together.

My embrace with the lady grew stronger as the light and sounds of the statue intensified. Eventually, I could not keep my eyes open and we buried our heads into one another's arms. When I began wondering how much longer I could endure, it stopped with such suddenness that I thought it might project me somewhere, but there was no sense of motion. My body was all I could feel. The lady and the world had vanished, like snowflakes on my hand.

I was floating in nothingness, but could not call it darkness, for I could see myself. I could make out no source of light, and found that my hands did not cast shadows on my body—as if I was the light that caused me to be visible. I looked around, but could make out nothing else. I wondered why I did not feel afraid. I was overwhelmed with the same sense of calmness that had been with me throughout the night, and patiently waited for whatever was to happen next. I enjoyed my weightlessness immensely, and felt like I could float forever. There was nothing to worry about. Time and space seemed completely absent.

Eight rings, hundreds of times my size, appeared in front of me. Their material was unknown to me, for it resembled many things—the fluidity of water or glass, the brilliant shimmer of polished metals, the reflective nature of mirrors—I could not decide.

They floated slowly, entangled and mixed, moving around and within each other, like a magician with his linking rings. The rings were guarding something. As soon as one rotated or moved out of the way, another would, in combination with the others, assist in blocking my view. Their rhythmic movements spun and spun until I found myself in the same familiar trance—the feeling of detachment and guidance combined. Of letting go entirely to unseen forces.

The rings continued in this manner, blocking whatever it was that I could not see for an unknown length of time until eventually they started revealing their secret. First, its corner, then, a part from the top, and I mentally kicked myself for not knowing sooner that it was obviously the statue of Ganesha. I crossed my arms, tilting my head back like Mr. T, and waited for the rings to assume the position.

They did, lining up one by one, creating a tunnel between the elephant and I, so perfectly in line that they seemed to become a single circle with Ganesha in the middle. I supposed I was going to float through the tunnel towards the statue, and began to think the whole thing rather corny and predictable when I did indeed begin to move in its direction.

Still curious, I passed through the tunnel of circles, inspecting each one as I passed.

When I stopped moving, I figured it would be best to say something, since it hadn't said anything at all, really. Floating before the statue, which I realized was much larger now then it had been in the museum, I thought for a bit, then smiled, shrugged my shoulders, and spoke.

"Well, gee, err . . . I guess I should thank you for this and all, and let you know that I'm ready for whatever it is you have to show me, or offer me or whatever."

I felt rather stupid. I was probably supposed to be doing some ritual that had been prepared and repeated for thousands of years. A "gee thanks, I'm ready" seemed rather insufficient.

It must have worked though, for an inaudible voice began talking in my head. It was a foreign language at first, which confused me so furiously I thought it might drive me insane, like the noise and light before. It began to tune in though, like listening to a crowd of people talking in a cocktail party. At first, I was unable to hear any one thing in particular, but then, just as one can hear their own name spoken in a crowd; I was able to focus on the voice. His voice sounded like Santa Claus—or at least what you'd expect—soft, old, soothing. Calmly, it spoke to me, as the Lady had whispered in my ear.

The truth is not declared directly, because everything in this universe is truth itself, and it is not the nature of mankind to find it, but to recognize it in themselves and other things.

I was completely captivated again, unable to speak or move. However, I would not have wanted to do either, for the voice felt better than anything I had ever felt before. Like the hands of a masseuse through my mind. A symphony within my heart. It continued.

It is in your nature to repeat the cycle of life until you understand this. All that holds you back is fear, within the arena of time and space. When it is dismissed, you will understand. I am giving you the opportunity, Phaedrus, to bypass this repeating cycle, for I have recognized you as a be-

ing that can handle a direct approach. Of course, you have many faults, but still, you are worthy.

The presence of the entity began to move away, manifesting an awful feeling of departure. A lover, leaving. Young children, taken from their parents. It was slow enough not to kill me, but also slow enough to make the whole thing agonizing. Removing a Band-Aid that covers a gash instead of a cut. Driving your love to an airport.

I will put you in the right place, at the right time, to witness the miracles that many do not get to see. I will always let you decide. The choice will always be yours.

The surrounding blackness turned lighter, resembling night. Again, I felt slightly idiotic when I looked down and realized that I was indeed within the night-sky, hovering above the Metropolitan.

You will not understand this all at first, but as the process continues, you will turn from novice to master. You will return now, with the following understanding: There will be a storm tonight, containing an element of my creation, sharper than a scalpel, smaller than a molecule. It could fall onto the street, returning to the earth it came from, or it could fall onto a human being, deftly passing into a specific place in their brain, causing them to react differently than they would have if it had never fallen from the sky. It can only pass through human matter, and will be deflected by anything else. Remember this, and that you will always have an opportunity to circumvent our destined unity. How long you take to reach me is all you must consider.

It was just as the lady in red had said before, but sounded so much more attractive now that I knew where I was heading. The voice departed then, and I was descending from the sky towards the stairs. They were still lined by the red carpet, and again I was reminded of a present, elaborately wrapped in red ribbon. However, the resemblance was even greater from my bird's eye view. Closer and closer I came, until I arrived on the steps in a standing position. I looked up into the sky, then down at the carpet I stood on. I rubbed my head, trying to regain some kind of connection with reality.

Trying to come out of this trance while being tackled by a guard made the whole process much more painful. Jumping into cold water after a hot bath, rather than just getting out and toweling off. He backed off as quickly as he had jumped onto me though, when I heard my father inform him that everything was okay. The security guard[17] started to apologize—"he seemed to have come out of nowhere sir . . . these things usually don't happen . . ."

"Quite alright officer. This is my son, Phaedrus. He just seems to have gotten a little lost. No need to worry. Have a good night."

The man helped me up and I nervously thanked him. I had no idea how to explain the situation, because I did not know exactly what had happened. My father's hands provided a firm, strong grip, which felt wonderfully comforting after floating in the cosmos. When I was standing on my feet again, he looked into my eyes. I assumed he was searching for signs of substance abuse, but instead, he pursed his lips, almost nostalgically.

"I never thought this day would come, Phaedrus, but it has, I'm only glad I was able to distract everyone in there before you vanished. You have no doubt been in touch with Ganesha by now, and given some kind of decree concerning the near future?"

I nodded my head in astonishment, having no idea how he could have known. My father seemed so simple, compared to

---

[17] It just so happens that the guard had been hired for security reasons from the Long Island police force, and particularly disliked adolescent youths. This was discovered by several acquaintances of mine when they went to a beach in Bridgehampton to burn their SAT practice books and applications after getting into college. The policeman was on duty, and told them that he had not been able to get into a decent school because of a poor SAT score.

He told them that because they had been trespassing and had tried to start a fire, he would take them in and report their arrests to the institutions they had just matriculated unless they scored above a 1400 on a practice test right there in front of him.

He pulled out his watch and began timing them. Luckily enough, they all passed with flying colors and were released.

the recent events, and to think that he had known what was happening all along created an entirely new perspective of him.

"Good then. No bother telling me the details—I'd rather not know them, but you can be sure we'll be in touch, and if you're ever in some kind of, oh, how should I say it *special* situation, give me a call. But for God's sakes, I won't be around to get you out of jail or anything, so don't get into any trouble."

"You are within the experience now. Nothing will ever be the same again. It is important that you know this."

I nodded again and watched him walk into a limousine, which promptly glided down Fifth Avenue towards the moon.

The guard was still looking at me rather suspiciously, and so I quickly stepped off the carpet and made my way back towards the side, where my friends would no doubt be on negative verses of their song. I sat down on the nearest bench, preferring solitude to their conformity. When one has too many things to think about, the eye of the storm is found sometimes, allowing peace within the mind. Although my conscious mind was ripping at the seems with objectivity, the familiar calmness returned, as if I was moving along with this eye, so as to watch the chaos of the storm around me while I stayed dry.

The sound of steps surprised me, and I looked up to find Antonia walking in my direction. She was apparently coming from the group that I had also left, for I had seen her there amongst my friends. She was the most attractive girl in the whole group, and I debated as to whether she was perhaps the most attractive girl I had ever seen. I will leave the description there, for who would be so arrogant to attempt the description of perfection?

I looked forward to the times I saw her, I looked even farther towards the times I actually talked to her, and beyond that I have not even tried to see, for ultimately my vision in the realm of such desirous girls was not so good. I could see that she was bothered though, and that something was obviously bearing down on her. Her shoulders hung so low the weight of her matters were almost visible—Her arms were tightly crossed, as if trying to support her body. An invisible hand held her head down, so that her chin bumped on her chest each time she stepped. Her purse hung low on one shoulder, hitting her thigh in rhythm with the stepping and the chin.

She would not have noticed if I had wanted to stay in solitude, but I felt the urge to talk. Perhaps the eye of the storm had room for two. I called her name when she was right in front of me, hoping to distract her enough to take away her worries. She was no doubt walking away from something, rather then towards any one thing at all.

I surprised her. Shoulders up, neck swinging, frown forgotten, smile recalled. She stood in front of me.

"Phaedrus! Where did you float off to?"

I began to laugh with my entire body until I started crying, and Antonia kept on trying to extract the joke from me. It finally seemed clear to her that attempts towards any explanation would be futile, and so she joined me in the laughter by laughing at me instead.

The more I calmed down, the closer she came to me, until we had found something of a balance in which I was still giggling, but by no means roaring anymore, and she was resting on the bench, but certainly not sitting on it either. She looked at me curiously, instinctively detecting that something significant had happened.

If there was to be any discussion at all, I was sure the topic would be regarding her, for I did not feel the need to tell her how I felt—it was obvious she sensed it. And so although we both were glad that she had temporarily forgotten, we knew that it would eventually be necessary to confront whatever was the matter.

"What's troubling you?" I asked, and watched her smile turn over at the same time her eyes did. A sigh, then

"I miss him so much, Phaedrus, that I don't enjoy the world when I'm not with him, and he is so far away, and it will be so long until I see him again, nothing feels right."

His name was Sammy Aldo, the man she had met in Sweden, whom I had had the opportunity of meeting once. I understood her longing, for he was indeed an astonishing character. He was a driven musician. A philosopher, a dreamer—all the things I saw within myself. To be reminded of the man called up a sense of longing, and just thinking about how awful it would be to have him as an absent lover created heaviness inside me.

She continued.

"So I'm thinking of breaking up, you know? I can't go on like this. I know why people say long distance relationships don't work now. Either way, I feel lost. I'm afraid the distance between us is really going to separate us. It's only a matter of time."

She sighed and continued to stare at the ground. My sympathy was growing with each breath she took. She was waiting for my response. Anything but the silence, for my lack of words implied the absence of solution. Realizing that each second emphasized her helplessness, I spoke.

"But every relationship has problems. The main one with yours is distance, other people are too close" She looked up, so I tried to keep on going "just think, if all you did was see him, don't you think it might become a problem?" Her eyes, returning to the ground, pondering the thought, caused me to realize I had said the wrong thing. Even I wish I could be that close to such a friendly person.

"What I mean to say is that the fact that Sammy lives so far away is just another test of how much you love him."

She didn't react. I sighed with frustration. I looked down at the ground as well, resting elbows on my knees, clasping my hands together. The bricks were only bricks to me, but to her I knew they were not there at all. Recollections of his wolf-like stares and movements painted the floor beneath her. I wished that I could see her thoughts, rather than the dull red bricks. I heard her choke, but could not bare to watch her cry, so kept my eyes upon the bricks, which slowly began to shine with teardrops.

I assumed that she was looking for a Kleenex in her bag, and was surprised to hear the mechanical unfolding of an umbrella. I realized that the tears did not belong to her at all, but to the sky above, which had been empty just moments ago. It caught me off guard, and the implications of the rain began to wash over my body even faster than the rain itself. Was this the rain Ganesha had prophesied? She stood up slowly, hunched over with the heavy heart.

"No, wait . . . you can't go yet." I said.

"Why not? It's raining. I don't want to get wet."

"Why not? What's wrong with being wet?"

"Are you crazy?"

"Come on" I said, "I have something to show you."

I guided her free hand towards the fountain, and the way she followed made her hesitation tangible in the resistance from her hand. I started talking out loud, fiercely this time, thinking of Sammy; wondering if someone was pulling him towards a fountain somewhere deep in Sweden. If someone was listening to a song he had written that expressed what he had felt through her, or if he was falling through the air on his snowboard somewhere, trying to reach her each time he left the snow.

"There were faithful lovers once—no, thousands—who couldn't see each other for years at a time . . . had no way of staying in touch, yet here you are, crying to me instead of him because I'm here and he isn't. But his voice is on the other end of a phone Antonia, his words are on a screen, and everything you said to one another could be recorded and replayed on tapes for a thousand others. And you think he's distant. You think he's distant because he isn't standing in front of you to accompany the love you feel for him but cannot touch. You want to touch the love you cannot feel."

I could see the rain cloud coming, felt it falling harder after leaving the bench and the trees that sheltered it. We reached the fountain and I stepped onto its rim so the water touched my heels, and the fountain was splashing up behind me, causing a moving wall to flow behind me. I was getting very wet, but Antonia kept on holding the rain to the umbrella.

"And now you want to give up because it's too hard for you. You can't handle such a petty thing as distance, and you know it. You hold on to the distance to excuse your physical needs.

"Maybe to you it just means getting wet and having to walk around in soaking clothes that make you cold and uncomfortable, but at least I can say I knew it was rain Antonia. I'm feeling it now, all around, and all you have is what you see and what you hear beneath that comfortable umbrella."

There was a flash of lightning, followed by a pause, then thunder as loud as the lightning was bright.

"It's water Antonia. You need it and you owe it everything, and yet you separate yourself from it when it doesn't seem convenient?"

Another flash of lightning, followed by a pause remarkably shorter than the first. I looked up at the sky, then down again. I could not interpret her expression. The water was falling off of me in large, heavy drops, falling in and out of rhythm with the drops from her umbrella. Like listening to the difference in the ticking of two clocks. I had nothing left to say.

I watched her fist move slowly towards the top of her umbrella, as if she had chosen to close it, but wanted to give her doubts time to think.

And then there was the lightning and the thunder at the same time.

Antonia closes umbrella: Go to chapter 101

Antonia keeps umbrella open: Go to chapter 342

Chapter 2

I felt like I had lost my senses for some time. I did not know how long I had lost my senses because I had lost my sense of time as well. I only knew that I had stepped into the tunnel and suddenly I was standing in a jacket and tie after regaining my senses, sitting in a chair. I appeared to be sitting in the hall of a hotel in front of two elevators. Everything was extensively decorated to the point where I wondered if perhaps this was a palace of some kind and not just some hotel. However, my instincts told me it was a hotel. It felt like there was something going on in this hotel, even though I could not hear or see anything.

I wondered if I was dreaming, or perhaps having some kind of vision.

If that is the case, I thought, this is so much like that place in Hiruko Murakami's novel "The Wind-Up Bird Chronicle" that I almost feel guilty, even though this is my dream.

A phone began to ring on a table next to me. Other than the fact that it was gold, there was nothing interesting or unique about the phone. I picked up the receiver.

"Hello?"

The monotone voice of an overworked operator responded,

"Office of the International Mime Association, how may I help you?"

"What? Sorry . . . I just picked up this phone. I'm in some kind of hotel—"

But before I could finish there was an audible clicking sound. She had hung up.

The elevators opened at the same time. Through the one on the left, I could see a part of my bedroom, and through the door on the right, I could see my bedroom, except slightly altered.

I got out of my chair and approached the open doors, trying to look into both of them and thus walking towards the center, until all I could see were the two images of my room growing larger and larger. The harder I looked, the less distinctive they became, and finally there was nothing but the one image of my room on every side of me. I realized that I was actually in my room. The hotel had disappeared.

Moving the curtains away from the window, I leaned my forehead on the glass, looking for my friends.

Go to chapter 0

Chapter 90

I was standing on the horizon. The greatest point of no return. Barely visible, let alone reachable. It was wet, like walking on the only edge of the ocean. Imagine water with corners and lines. A wet geometry . . . hydrogeometry, if you will. Balancing myself upon this structure, I quickly learned that it was not too hard to move back and forth. However, it was not possible to move sideways. I assumed this was because if I did, I would no longer be on the horizon.

Figures approached and passed by, but I could never get a good look to see what they were. They disappeared somehow, as if I was watching them fade in the distance while adjacent to them at the same time. Now and then I saw what must have been horses—even a car occasionally. There might have been couples, embracing, holding hands. It was useless though—like trying to define the shapes of moving clouds.

And as thoughts wander like the herds of clouds along the sky while observing them from down below, so did my own. I imagined what the moon might look like in the nighttime, for I could not see it where I stood—nor the sun. A perpetual dusk, if one could call it that.

Maybe if those really were cars passing by, I could hitch a ride somewhere.

A few moments before I would have started worrying, a voice distracted me from panic.

"So many people thought I was a genius in my lifetime, but from this viewpoint, it makes me wonder just how little I actually knew. Perhaps this explains my fear of audiences."

It was Albert Einstein, immediately recognizable by the hair and accent. I introduced myself as we shook hands. We continued to watch the obscured objects pass across our border. I felt that perhaps I was being impolite by standing in front of him, but could think of no way to switch positions.

"We are watching happy endings." He said.

"Is that what they are?"

"Yes. Heroes galloping off into the distance. Lovers holding hands as they walk away from their respective stories. Thelma and Louise, driving off a cliff'

"You're dead, and I'm here, with you. Does that mean I'm dead too?"

"Oh no, there's no need to worry about a thing like that. It's just that I died with the whole 'universe-thing' figured out pretty well, so I've been granted some special privileges."

"Like a backstage pass."

"Sure" He said, clearly not knowing what I was talking about. Our hands were in our pockets and an awkwardness followed that I did not know how to fill. I'm sure you can imagine how I felt, standing on *the* horizon, with *the* Albert Einstein. What could I have brought up to such a man? Luckily, he filled the silence.

"It appears to be a straight line, and it just disappears . . ." he said, looking down the line of the horizon. No one in the real world would ever look at the vertical line that was perpendicular to the horizon.[18] And if they could do that, I bet they couldn't do it next to Albert Einstein.

" . . . no wonder they thought the Earth was flat, or that space was linear."

"Yeah."

There was a poster once, hanging on the walls in the physics lab of my old high school, which read "Perfection is not a destination, it is a direction." But where was the truth in that if I was standing in a place that couldn't be reached with a dead man who had illustrated relativity?

"Do not be so conceited, Mr. Dumai, as to think you have reached perfection. Circles, remember? Waves? Cycles? This place, although theoretically impossible to reach, is nothing put a pretty little picture, drawn by the hands of some infantile deity with finger paint, in a nursery school of some divine community that we have yet to reach. We are only on

---

[18] See Illustration 5

the greatest point of no return that man knows, but there is no such thing for greater beings."

I wanted to know how he had read my mind, but realized that to be surprised would be a wasted effort on my part. He began to walk away.

"Come, I will show you something now."

"Okay."

He walked, hands still in his pockets, probably doing some incomprehensible equation in his head. I had abandoned curiosity a long time ago—so far, it had only lead me to pathetic expectations. I focused instead on the image ahead—walking along the horizon behind Einstein, on a thin line that felt like the tops of two waterfalls flowing out of one other.

I examined the sky, never having seen it so clearly. The rays of light were bending in various directions, composing the aria of colors above.

Einstein eventually reached a tall woman, who I recognized as the lady in red from the museum banquet, her strangely archetypal face and body giving contrast to the naturalistic impression that the horizon gave off. She saw me over the top of Einstein's head.

"I'd hug you," she said, "But Einstein's in the way."

"Oh, no trouble at all, I assure you!" He replied. Old man smile. Dirty but somehow clean because this was Einstein. She crossed her arms. No misconceptions. She still had the peanut. Einstein turned around to look at me. The lady wrapped her arms about him, twirling the toothpick that held the peanut with her right hand. Einstein took it from her, then turned back around towards me. We both jumped when he began to shell it and put it in her mouth. He noticed our concern over the fact that he had just eaten the peanut (the same thing I had almost done, I might add) only after chewing and swallowing.

"What?" He said, probably feeling the same way I did before she had stopped me in the museum.

"That," She said, "Was our young friend's ticket home."

If Einstein was concerned about this fact, he certainly was not showing it. He began to pick his teeth with the toothpick.

"This is where the members of the Polyversity club cross over. You are here, Phaedrus, because you have reached a point of no return--you can go one way, following the heroes and couples that we have seen into the unknown land beyond, where all the different elements of your adventure come back together, or you can go backwards, in order to see what could have been . . . these elements I talk of. You entered a universe composed entirely of you, and it has blossomed, like Buddha's blooming lotus. But perhaps you have only seen one of its petals? Consider how many petals you have on your lotus, before you make your decision, for wouldn't it be tragic if the trees within your orchard didn't have so many leaves?"

Other Petals: Go to chapter 0

Heroes and Couples: Go to Part II

Chapter 101

In my frenzied state I could not bare the intensity with which she moved her hands, and though they may have been the most random or significant handful of seconds in *your* life, they seemed to last eternally for me. You could have been driving on an interstate, or sleeping in your lover's arms. You could have been trying to remember why you walked into a room, or thinking of something to say when a conversation fell silent. I don't know where you were, but somewhere in your lifetime, or perhaps the lifetime of an ancestor, everyone's progress through time was surely much faster than my observation of Antonia's umbrella and the coming of a prophecy.

My experience with eternal suspense only added to the feeling of relief when the strength I had tried to find within her surged out faster than the wall of water behind me. She did not even bother to refold the umbrella, letting it simply swing off over her head until it was upside-down on the pavement.

She pushed me into the water, and jumped in after me. I did not try to find my balance. I only made sure I cradled her body as we fell into the fountain. My arms found balance for the both of us upon the fountain floor, slipping occasionally on the vast array of pennies that pedestrians had thrown into as dreams and wishes. I watched her splash around, then took the umbrella and brought it in with us. She sat in front of me, letting me use the umbrella to scoop up the water and delicately pour it over her head.

"See? It's just water."

"Yes, just water."

And we played in the fountain, listening to nothing but our voices and the water as it fell around us.

We must have been a sight to see, heading downtown towards sixty ninth street, laughing and dripping all over the street. The world thought we were drunk, no doubt, and I agreed with them, except for the fact that it was not alcohol seeping through our veins, but only the realization that nothing really mattered, and we would eventually dry off.

She used her key to let us in, and we undressed by the front door, so as not to get the floors of her brownstone wet. I had been there a few times before, but had never realized how beautiful the place was until then. Polished floors, immaculate glass, furniture most likely built for palaces somewhere in Britain, a cocker spaniel with a droopy face that spilled love through saliva and a tail wagging as seamlessly as the drops of water that fell from our own clothes. She passed me a towel and gym clothes to replace the soaking laundry I had worn into the fountain.

We went upstairs when were sufficiently. The cocker spaniel gaily climbed the stairs with us, nearly tripping me over each step I took. Up we went, higher and higher into the house, which was tall and thin, so each floor seemed a different section of the house entirely—the dining room floor, the living room floor, the master bedrooms. We reached the floor that held her room and her sister's room.

I smiled and told her I was going to get something to drink, to which she smiled and requested that I also fetch a gin and tonic for her. So back downstairs I went, while the spaniel hugged my legs in total excitation as I got closer to the kitchen. However, I stopped my descent upon passing the floor that held her living room and what seemed to be the library. I heard voices. Whispered tones that held the impression of secrecy and longing. Perhaps it was the man Antonia had been speaking about upstairs, I thought, and decided to investigate. I knew Antonia would be enamoured with her lover's voice for quite some time, and so did not feel any urgency to bet upstairs. I gripped the handle of the banister, leaning my ear to the edge of the wall, getting as close as I could without being seen.

" . . . A predicament indeed Simon, You may stay here as long as you wish, for of course *I* know you're innocent. The truth is though, I don't know how else I can help you. You *could* inquire with our mutual Ashta, who I'm sure could be of some assistance, but other than that I—"

The dog must have given me away, for it was sitting at the entrance to the library in a sitting position, anxiously awaiting my next step." In an effort to keep from seeming suspicious, I continued down the stairs, looking at it, saying "No, my dear, I'm not going to get you any food, I'm getting your owner drunk, that's all."

Putting on my best expression of surprise, I looked into the library, where Antonia's father was standing with a glass of Brandy, and the head of a rather short man peeked at me around a large chair.

"Well, what a nice surprise!" He exclaimed, "It's Kyo's son, Phaedrus! Please, do come in! I'm sure you'll be happy to meet my old friend Simon Cryptus, who I'm sure you've heard of before."

The small man rose from his chair and I slowly entered in astonishment. My eyes must have been wide enough to show my amazement, for they both laughed a little.

"*The* Simon Cryptus?" I asked, "The *'Schematics of Intrigue'* Simon Cryptus?"

"That's me," He said nervously.

I was too weakened by surprise to give him a strong shake, and he too seemed lacking in strength. Although he was smiling and seemed glad enough to meet me, there were heavy bags below his eyes, and—like Antonia—seemed weighted down. Simon Cryptus was my hero. A famous mystery writer I had started reading in my youth. He looked exactly as I imagined he would, with a face rather reminiscent of a mouse and a twitchy nose that added to this effect. He had short hair, cropped in a Caesar-style below the crown of his head to disguise his partial baldness.

I exchanged formalities with Antonia's father, who inquired about my own father, who he had known in boarding school. He did not bother to offer me a glass of Brandy, just put one in my hands and motioned for me to sit down.

"Perhaps Kyo's son might be of some assistance Simon. He wants to be a writer, and from what I hear, is a rather intelligent boy."

I smiled sheepishly, trying to push away the compliment.

"I would be honored to help you Mr. Cryptus, although I doubt I could think of anything useful."

"Oh don't be foolish Phaedrus," Simon said, "A fresh mind can always be of some assistance."

Antonia's father sat down in his large leather couch, crossed his legs, and took a sip of brandy before speaking. I did the same, letting the warmth of it seep down to my stomach.

"Simon's wife died last month."

Simon looked at him, then over at me.

"My condolences, Mr. Cryptus."

"Simon, please."

"Simon has been taken completely by surprise—and the fact that she is famous has not helped him deal with it.[19] The coroner's have no idea how she died. Simon found her in the morning sitting on the living room couch. Her heart had simply stopped beating.

Simon sipped his Brandy and looked over the armrest of the chair that seemed to be engulfing him. The Cocker Spaniel had sat down beside his chair, and Simon affectionately patted its head while listening to his friend's narration.

"And although everyone knows they were very much in love, it seems the New York Department of Law Enforce-

---

[19] Simon's first reaction was a suicide attempt, although he never admitted afterwards. He had tried to drown himself in his bath with a toaster, but had been resuscitated by the paramedics. After recovering, he had gone back to the hospital which he had been brought to, and shouted at a Doctor named Alison (whose last name I will not divulge) who had saved his life. He asked her how she had dared to keep him from something which had seemed so important to him, and the ethical debate that ensued was enough to seriously confuse her.

While walking home from work the next day, a piece of refuse fell off of a crane onto her head and killed her. Coincedentally, Simon Cryptus had been walking on the same block, and came to her in hope of helping her. He had wanted to apologize for screaming at her in the hospital, but had to do so in the street in the short amount of time before she died.

"I understand now," he said, "I'm sorry."

Although her death was tragic, Simon Cryptus knew her death had happened for a good cause, and was never again angered by the attempts that caring people made to interrupt another person's life.

ment is very suspicious. Of course, Simon appears to be completely innocent, but this is no normal man we are talking about. This is Simon Cryptus, master of mystery and crime writing. Compared by critiques to Sir Arthur Conan Doyle and the likes."

Now it was Simon's turn to blush as I had, beneath his words of admiration.

"If anyone could pull off a murder, it would no doubt be the man before us. Consequentially, the law has taken it upon them to make sure they won't be fooled. Unfortunately for them, Simon did not kill her. Unfortunately for Simon, everyone is suspicious."

I smiled as much as it seemed appropriate to, without being impolite.

"How ironic." I said.

"That's Simon Cryptus for you." Antonia said, who surprised us all by appearing in the same way I had on the edge of the entry-way, elevated by the steps. She said it with a little humor, but realized no one was really laughing. She came in and greeted Simon with an affectionate kiss on the forehead. Calmly striding towards the bar to pour herself a drink.

"So the question Phaedrus, is what to do now."

Antonia sat next to me on the couch. I could tell she was dying to tell me something, but was being polite not to interrupt the conversation. Simon's eyes rested on me as he reclined in the massive chair. I breathed in the Brandy, exhaled, and spoke. It was, for me, a moment not unlike those everyone experiences in which one knows he had better say something, and whatever it is, it had better be good.

"It seems to me like you have a wonderful opportunity Simon. You get to mind-fuck the world, and every artist dies for such a chance. If you are innocent, you have nothing to hide, and the investigators can take all the time they want to inspect you. The public will react just as much to your writing as they will to your subsequent actions, consequentially making you yourself into an object of your own creation."

Simon responded as soon as I had finished by abruptly moving forward to me.

"Yes of course, that was my first idea too. But how can I go about my life when everyone around me thinks I'm a murderer? My quality of life is in the ruins, I know I'll have my freedom, but what am I supposed to do with it?"

"I think that's a matter of how you want to live your life. Whether or not you want to live in fear or not. You say your friends know you are innocent, so what should it matter what everyone else thinks? The world is now your toy."

Simon leaned back in his chair while Antonia's father stayed silent. He had been silent while I spoke to Simon, and hadn't moved when I was speaking. Antonia broke the silence.

"Aren't you the positivc role model tonight. Encouraging me with Sammy, helping Simon with the same words. What happened to you? Come on, let's go upstairs and talk."

I politely said goodbye to them, which didn't get much of a reaction. Both seemed somewhere deep in thought, infinitely far away from Antonia and me. I wanted to stay with them in the library--to discuss the different connotations of Simon's paradoxical reality and the different ways he might escape his maze. However, Antonia had other ideas and she dragged me upstairs with her right hand and the flask of Brandy in her left.

She closed the door once we were both inside as soon as I had my last foot in from the hallway. Antonia didn't even give her hands the time to close it, giving the job instead to her feet as she poured two more glasses of Brandy and shoved them into my hands. She did this so quickly that the dog did not have time to enter behind her and almost lost its nose.

I assumed she was excited by her recent conversation with Sammy, but a further inspection of her gleaming eyes told me that something more had transgressed. She was swallowing her Brandy as if it were water, with a smile on her face that seemed to reflect the liquor, mixing with her thoughts.

But suddenly, someone was knocking on the door, and we were both refilled with a different kind of anticipation. She approached the door and let her father in, followed by Simon. They both stood in the center of the room, appearing out of place in the bedroom of an adolescent girl.

"Simon and I came to the realization just after the two of you left, that Sammy and you might be pondering a membership with the Polyversity Club, and I don't want you to make any decisions that you haven't fully considered. Simon and I have also discussed the idea, and think it might also be an option for him. I want you to understand how different it is for him then it would be for Sammy. You cannot take this decision lightly."

Antonia looked towards the ground, somewhat shamefully, and I'm sure I looked confused.

"This being said, both Simon and I think it would be a good idea to get Phaed—"

"I was just about to ask him dad."

Simon and her father looked at me, just like parents must before they tell their children the facts of life. Letting them in on a completely mysterious part of the world that all the grown-ups know about.

" . . . After all, he is a good family friend, and has already proven to be an extremely intelligent and beneficial young man."

Simon stepped forward.

"I think it would be extremely beneficial to the world in general if you had access to the club. It seems you are motivated towards directing other people—not just yourself—in the right direction, and this is exactly what is needed."

They both paused, looking at the two of us in a proud manner, as if finally relieved of something they had both been worrying about. Her father spoke in a hushed, dramatic tone, then lead Simon out the door.

"Yes . . . exactly what it needs. Antonia, fill him in on the details. I'll have some more drinks sent up, and then we'll all meet back in the den. Simon and I have some things to arrange."

They left. I didn't have to do anything to get Antonia to explain, she just did, looking back at me with the same smile and poured another glass of Brandy from flask to glass to throat in one consecutive motion.

"We think it started somewhere with the Greeks, because that's where Tragedy began, isn't it? I'm not really sure, some of the members are really into the historical aspects, so you can ask them if you're interested. Anyway, there was this ritual created a really long time ago, for people who needed to escape reality."

"Escape to where?"

"Shut up" She refilled my glass "Just keep drinking and listening, alright? They created a loophole somehow, in the world, and people who are so inclined can become what they call 'chair members' of the club, which is basically just a cover for saying that they're the ones the club exists for. You know that movie that always comes on around Christmas? It's a Wonderful Life? Well it's kind of like that. People can choose to never have existed at all, except that all of their influences remain the same, which means that everyone remembers who they are and what they did. In this way, they can escape reality by entering an alternate reality in which they never disappeared. Using the comparative analysis of other club members who are not 'chair members' they can decide which reality to exist in. Depending on their circumstance, they can furthermore manipulate the loophole so that they have a ton of available options. They can come back from their disappearance in our reality, they can go on in the other reality, they can erase their existence completely in this one, they can go back in time and make it look like they died, there's really no limit."

"So you're saying that through this club, different universes are created each time one of these experiments take place?"

I was entranced now, and it seemed Antonia was also surprised by her own clarity, as though it was suddenly all making sense for the first time.

"No, I'm saying that we merely tap into the different universes that are created each time they come into existence. Some universes are small, maybe just a passing thought, and others are entire creations made by the minds of artists and the people of the world. When you create a thought, it exists somewhere, and therefore has mass. Because of relativity, this mass is energy and the energy is power. We are in a universe, meaning, one verse. In truth, there are many verses, so they call it the Polyversity Club. The club documents everything that has already been done, but new combinations and ideas are constantly materializing. Sometimes it's from members of the club, sometimes it's from the outside world, we just make sure the club is handled in an organized fashion."

I refilled my glass and proposed the question I had been wanting to ask during the last part of her explanation.

"This has something to do with Ganesha, doesn't it?"

"Who?"

"The God that looks like an elephant?"

"That's the one. There's a statue of him in the club."

"I should speak to your father now."

So we picked up the Brandy again and migrated back to the den. By that time I was starting to feel it. It was a wonderful feeling though, lacking sickness or dizziness. It was as though opium and brandy had mated and given birth inside my stomach, allowing everything to feel increasingly bizarre while keeping away any paranoia through the Brandy's relaxing qualities. On our way downstairs Antonia said "By the way, this isn't Brandy we've been drinking all night."

"What is it?"

"It's this Exotic Liquor that the club imports. I think it's called *Drolunsivo* or something, but everyone calls it Elephant Cocoa."

I paused for a second, deciding that the pleasant effect from the drink outweighed the fact that I had been deceived. I even appreciated the gesture in a way, because the men had served it to me the moment I had entered.

"By the way Antonia, what is your father's name?"

"Michael."

Simon and Michael were standing in the room, looking at the fire. Antonia was about to say something, but I squeezed her shoulder and spoke first.

"I was contacted by Gnesh in the museum tonight, before running into Antonia. He gave me a short-term prophecy, which came true during the thunderstorm tonight. It affected the way in which Antonia thought. I thought it the proper decision. It's obvious my presence here is not a coincidence. I thought you should know this before we go on."

Michael formed an 'o' with his mouth and let out a sigh that eventually rested in a smiling position. Simon stepped back and crossed his arms and looked satisfied. Michael raised his glass into the air.

"Well then, we had better go then. The sooner the better."

We did not hesitate at the door, passing on into the street as if the staircase had never ended—the difference between inside and outside being completely insignificant. An antique Rolls Royce awaited us directly outside, which Michael and her daughter marched into without looking away from the car.

Although there were two rows of seats inside the car we all crowded onto the same side, so that we were going forward when the car began to move. It was a tight fit, but comfortable.

After some silence, Michael breathed in heavily, as if everyone had been patiently waiting for him to talk. Antonia interrupted before he could start though.

"Daddy, didn't the Greeks say we were moving through time backwards because we could see the past, but not the future?"

"Yes, dear, they did."

Silence again, and we all sat looking at the empty seats for awhile before Michael took another breathe and, because Antonia was shorter than us both, spoke to me over her head.

"I know this whole experience feels strange, but that's only because you aren't used to taking such a direct course into the heart of things. Life is usually much slower. It takes some getting used to. If you ever need a breather, just avoid the right direction. Don't you think that's what people do in life when the truth is too bright? They need to look away. Let their eyes adjust. I'm saying this because it only gets weirder. The destination's still the same if you decide to take a longer route. It's also important for you to know something before we introduce you to the club. I admit, we didn't recognize you at first, but now it seems obvious to us why Gnesh chose you. Everyone is going to realize it, some faster than others. You see, the club has been anticipating something that will help us assist the world take the next step. I don't know how to describe it to you, because I don't fully understand myself. I'm sure though, that you will come to understand it more than any of us. So if people seem somewhat persistent, it's only because we've been expecting someone like you for a few months now, and we were getting somewhat worried."

I chuckled and said,

"My father said the museum had had some problems getting the artifact all the way over here. I guess deadlines in reality even mess up plans of the gods sometimes."

"Actually, no, you're completely wrong."

"Oh."

"That is what we're curious about though. Gnesh is the remover of obstacles. Sometimes when we're joking around we call him the deity of no delay. We know there's some reason behind his late arrival, but no one knows what it is. We all assume that it's being kept secret for our safety, but still, even tricksters like ourselves get curious. Wait, no, let me rephrase that. Tricksters like us suffer more from curiosity then normal people. It is in our nature to react against the bliss of ignorance. Like an allergy. It is the world's opium, and our poison. This explains our nature of curiosity and our desire to show other people what we have discovered."

We all fell silent again. Simon was twiddling his thumbs, but twiddling is an understatement, for the way in which each thumb coiled around its mate was so entrancing it reminded me of DNA strands. Double helixes. Motion so smooth within a simplistic, finite system, I could not take my eyes away. Perhaps this had happened so as not to know our route, or maybe I had just become distracted by the enigmatic traits of Simon Cryptic.

The car door opened once we had stopped but I was unable to see the other streets. Canopies hooded the path inside, but I did not feel the urge to look around. I felt overwhelmed with curiosity. To know a loved one thought of you.

There was a doorman, dressed appropriately, with a rather outdated hat and a face to match. He smiled to Michael, then after momentarily observing the rest of us, opened the door before we reached it so we did not have to stop.

If Antonia's house had been expanded to the form of a castle, it would have resembled the club. Chandeliers hung from the ceiling and polished marble floors revealed or reflection. Not slippery but light, giving one the sense they had been polished by clouds instead of wax and that walking on them was not to walk on them at all, but to skate upon the silver lining of a cloud. Two magnificent staircases connected either side of the room to the same second level. All that felt eerie was the lobby's emptiness. The quietness that should have been replaced by busy socialites that talked over champagne and cocktails

But they did not give me time to pause, and before I had any time at all to inspect the grand entrance, we were walking downstairs through a hallway thin enough to force us into single-file progression. The farther we descended, the volume of laughter and chattering increased, and before I was ready, we had entered the Club's real lobby, rather than the relatively unappealing one upstairs. Cheap, comfortable. The perfect place to stay. One might compare it to a hole within the wall that had been decorated almost too well. The colors had been carefully applied without an inclination towards designs or complications. Only what felt right, in the right place, with its inhabitants to compliment their personal backgrounds.

We passed the statue of Gnesh, which no one else seemed to notice.

Down we went, through flights of stairs into a crowded room of people.

I checked out the bar while Michael and his daughter did a round amongst the members. There were card tables and Backgammon boards, shelves full of books impossible to read. I gathered my courage and disguised myself as one who did not fear rejection—ambivalent towards the crowd.

There were many people in that room. Faces that I recognized, with no idea as to how I'd met them, like attending a high school reunion full of people you passed in the hallways and whose names were never even clear to you when you were in school, let alone then.

I was looking around, trying to loose the sense of discomfort that everyone gets from crowds of people who already know one another, when a couple appeared in front of me, apparently eager to see me after such a long time of separation. I did not recognize them at first, but the way they interacted with one another--the sense of rhyme between the them--quickly gave their identities away.

"Romeo? Juliette? This is so incredible! How did you end up here?"

The couple gazed into each other and eventually regained eye contact with me.

"Mercutio! Have you been fortunate to find this place as well?"

Their faces had certainly rung bells within my head, but it was the sound of his voice that made me truly remember. It was indeed the famous couple, taking a break from the dance-floor, Juliette in tow, dressed with a sense of elegance that made me feel inadequate.

We sat down at a table. Waiters offered glasses of champagne on silver trays, oblivious to my desire for sobriety. I politely declined, but Romeo would have nothing of it, standing up ferociously to wave the liquor-baring servant away.

"Oh leave him alone you Tybalt of today! Can't you see my friend has purged you from our lives? He doesn't want to drink!"

Juliette tugged his hand back down towards the table, and he quickly forgot. Having done no harm at all, the servant left with his champagne.

I had no idea what was going on. Hadn't they died in each other's arms? Hadn't they become a thought to mourn upon in melancholy moments? Yet recollections of our friendship consumed me. I remembered the stories he had told me about the coffee stain that splashed over his torso, which he had inherited by means of an immaculate tattoo that Picasso had drawn upon his mother. A tattoo so moving and so beautiful that it had left a mark beyond her skin, down into the depths of DNA.

I could not understand the ways in which these memories were coming to me, for it seemed as though the lover that we know as Romeo had somehow come to hold these strange positions in my memories[20]. As though Romeo had never

---

[20] The Romeo that none will ever know, who I met at the Polyversity club as if we had been friends for a long time, has an interesting story. No one ever read Shakespeare's greatest piece until his great great grandson—the alternate Romeo—found it in his final manuscript that he had placed in between completely unrelated reference books on the very highest shelf in the corner of an isolated tower which had been his private library.

He had recently inherited the castle from his father, around the time of a great war being waged in England. It had taken months to renovate, but Romeo eventually moved in and had become free to explore the mansion at his leisure. He took to coming down from his office—located in a different tower—with a glass of sherry in his left hand and walk through different sections of his enormous home. Through these fascinating, sleepless nights, the house's secret history revealed itself, which made him feel as if the place was somehow growing comfortable with him.

He found the poem during one of these excursions. Because the night had been so clear and the stars so bright, nothing could have seemed more appropriate than to try and use the antique telescopes. He eventually gave up though, for rust had caused their blindness. He was glad in fact, that they did not work. He favored the stars as a whole, rather than one at a time. Content with this result of fruitless telescopes, he had entered the library and started going through the books.

The manuscript was considerably fragile. The poem on the final page had almost fallen into pieces, but Romeo had been lucky; A long piece of braided hair had been tied into the book, like some kind of place-keeper, helping the tired paper stay together as it turned in Romeo's hands. He had been standing on the highest possible rung on the library's moving ladder, going through the books while keeping his balance. He had taken the manuscript down to the desk as soon as he realized what it was.

It was a series of sonnets, pertaining to the twin daughters of Rapunzel, who had been named Herponnie and Tayle. Romeo's famous ancestor had believed that his castle had belonged to the prince who saved Rapunzel, and was actually the home in which they lived 'happily ever after.' Romeo was on his third glass of cherry and had read the poem many times before realizing that the braided hair was actually covering the final verses.

The most intriguing thing about Rapunzel's children, apparently, was that they were Siamese twins. When they were born, everyone thought they were joined at the scalp. But Rapunzel, her prince, and the subjects of their kingdom soon discovered that this was not the case—they were bound together by their hair. The doctor's and scientists of the kingdom would have separated them immediately if there had not been superstition that doing this might kill them. So their hair grew out and as years passed they were able to stand further and further apart. Their hair was braided and displayed. The prince convinced the people that it was a miracle from God—that his kingdom had been blessed.

Before the prince died, he split his kingdom in half and left half of it to Herponnie and half of it to Tayle. Because they could not reign their land without living in it, he decided to make the border between the two halves within the castle, in the bedroom that his daughters shared. They would walk around their room, moving back and forth between the two territories, ruling justly and fairly until they died together, having lived their lives without ever leaving the other's presence. They named their land by listening to their favorite bird-songs on the morning of their father's death.

Romeo had known his castle lied somewhere on the border between the two countries, but had no idea that he was *precisely* on the border. If the poem was true, it was possible that he had been crossing the border many time a day—perhaps even in his sleep, if his bed was in the right place.

Romeo thought until dawn. He smoked a cigar and finished off his cherry. Although the sun had started shining and the stars had disappeared, he moved into the port. When it became a reasonable hour, he moved into his own office and started making the appropriate calls. During the night, he had experienced a transformation in which he realized the fact that his financial success meant nothing. After managing to flee Verona with his soul-mate, there had never been a real purpose.

The deeper he searched, the farther back the mansion went in history and the more it became entangled with the politics of international borderlines. But in the end it was clear—his mansion lied right on the border.

died, and the very essence of his being had been capable of living through the past and on into my present.

Romeo saw that I was baffled by their presence before me and within my mind. He whispered in his lover's ear, then tried half-heartedly to justify their presence.

"All tragedies have other endings. All sadness turns to happiness in some way or another. So here we are, as if we had never died at all, and just as good things evolve and overcome old obstacles, old obstacles develop too, and turn into lessons of an increasingly complex nature."[21]

This being said, I looked around the room and suddenly began to recognize each person. Antonia, with her band of family and friends, began to introducc mc. Oedipus, Hamlet, Phaedra . . . I cannot recall each person, but a sense of happiness came over me, for the characters who had suffered such misfortune in their stories had found a place to make amends with every tragic message that their tales had illustrated.

I approached Antonia and took her from a cordial conversation as politely as possible and softly whispered in her ear.

Neither state had jurisdiction, and so the mansion stayed there under no one's laws except his own.

He knew then that the mansion had a special role within his destiny. The war was producing many people who wanted desperately to cross the borders, and though Romeo knew he could not help them all, he would try to help as many as he could.

He hired a butler and servants, and threw parties for the rich. They would invite important friends in need of help. It became the greatest and most secret way for any man to move between these territories, and because it was so hidden—like an unseen area of skin contained within the wrinkles of an old man's face—it attracted trickster heroes and mysterious agents, who would mix together in the night, producing many strange occurrences. The attic became a den in which the most important secrets were exchanged by spies disguised as mimes.

His guests would pay respect to him, passing from the South into the North or back by standing up from couches in his living room and passing to the dining room. They left from the opposite end of the house, onto another hemisphere of war.

[21] See Illustration 4

"How can such people be here? These are the figures of stories I have only read, that people created in their minds and then transcribed to paper . . . to canvases and songs, but not to such a state as this! How can this be happening?"

She put her hand upon my shoulder, smiling as I stared into her eyes with obvious confusion.

"Every thought, every idea, takes a form somewhere, no matter how small. And for the tragedies, for the people who deserve an alternate existence, Gnesh created this society: an oasis for the inspirations that have changed so many people's hearts. These characters can't just die. They have to go somewhere. This is where they come."

Shakespeare's lovers came and joined me with Antonia, who they had known since she was born. As we talked, I began to notice certain stares from people in the room, and although it gave me great discomfort, the company of perfect lovers eased my trepidation. Juliette continued smiling at her lover, while Antonia continued waving to the other members. It is times like these in which a person may feel lonely, even in the company of many people, for even while observing the others around me, I could not even find someone to share eye contact with.

This is when I ought to leave, I thought to myself, before I make a fool out of myself or let them down.

I saw a painting on the wall. After seeing such a vast array of different things, it felt good to witness something stationary. Within the wooden frame a picture had been painted of a sunset, slowly sinking into the horizon. It did not look unique at all, appearing just as full of color as a poster in a waiting room or the postcards from foreign destinations that were all too easily forgotten. The line depicting the horizon, however, seemed unusual to me, and as my eyes looked into it I felt as though I nearly saw the curve of the world within the line that had first looked straight.

Escape by leaving: Go to chapter 69
Escape by sitting still and looking into the horizon: Go to chapter 90

Chapter 69

I did not know that I had not yet met the most important member of the club.

He might have been sitting by the entrance all along, or perhaps he had never been there at all, just like everyone else in there. I had stood up from the table and immediately seen him with a gigantic book, writing continuously from right to left, as if writing in Hebrew, or letters to a mirror. He did not have to look directly, for he wore a pair of glasses in the shape of glass triangles—prisms--causing his vision to bend in a ninety degree angle.

I only meant to look at him for a brief time, as one does in stations or busy city streets, but I was unable to remove my stare. Upon looking at him though, I found that I could see much more than just a strange old man, writing at the table by the door. My sight was accompanied by several memories I did not recognize to be my own, yet they felt distinctly personal, in the same way I had found Romeo and Juliet upon arriving.

I saw a shopping mall in Kansas with a great glass ceiling which was so high up a tropical garden with trees and falling water had been planted in the center of the complex. However, the atmosphere was somewhat hampered by the mall, full of customers, pushing strollers, carrying shopping bags, talking on cellular phones, eating fast-food with the speed of America. A disturbing juxtaposition. It felt as though the club of missing people had vanished completely, giving way to this vision, rather than merely losing myself in memory.

The tables from the club were the same, except they now made up the eating area for various junk food outlets, where hungry consumers were sitting to fill their stomachs. However, the man was still visible and was sitting at the same table. I wondered if I was looking at the content of his writings. But if that was so, wouldn't everything be moving backwards?

I was sitting down with him then, with no recollection of having moved at all. He had a long beard. Long hair. Dirty clothes. Very generic in his appearance as an old—perhaps ancient—man. Appearing to be just a little younger than DaVinci's self-portrait. Definitely more hair. Because of the prism glasses, he did not need to bend his neck or back, and could write with perfect posture. He looked as if he were blind, reading braille with a pen instead of writing.

He paused and bent his head towards the ceiling so that he could see me. I could see his eyes in the prisms. It felt rather strange to know he was looking at me even though he was facing the ceiling. He held a V5 Pilot Precise with Rolling ball pen in his hand, which he offered to me without speaking.

"I use the same pen" I said, "they're my favorite."

"I agree. You can even see the ink through the side."

"Exactly! And the metal clasp on the top is so easy to use."

He smiled, clipping the pen onto the neck of his shirt.

"It appears we have much in common."

"And I love your glasses , they must make it so much easier to work."

"This is true. However, I can never remove them."

He continued.

"Long ago, I played a game of cards with the arc-angel, Gabriel. Because we could not gamble, we decided to make the game interesting by switching perspectives. He played his hands as a young, aspiring writer who dreamed of success, and I played as the messenger of God."

"Who won?"

"We didn't keep score. It was strictly for fun. Actually, now that I think about it, I don't think angels ever keep score when they play games. Anyway, the game ended, but I was never able to look at anything directly, for if I did, I would recognize the face of God in everything I saw, which would quickly lead to insanity."

"And Gabriel?"

"He was never able to look at his job with the same contentedness, for he had learned what it was to aspire."

I squinted, eager to appear as impressed as I felt. After letting this sink in, he brought his head back so he was looking at the book again. He flipped the pages, searching for a certain page.

"But I have not introduced myself to feed my own self-sympathy. I have brought us together so that you might expand you knowledge of the things you are destined to learn. I have accepted my fate—accepted it long ago. Unlike you and the majority of Earth's inhabitants , I have already seen the face of God, and have thus dedicated the remainder of my existence to recording the details of his face as explicitly as possible. If all you know is God, you will never be able to explain it to others. You will find yourself writing forever, trying to explain the memory of his countenance, defining the wrinkles of his cheeks in ever-increasing detail, like the scientist doomed to know more and more about less and less. I have met you to show the importance of comparing each face with that of God's, rather than only inspecting his. Every other face contains a part of his, and by learning to recognize them, you will be able to achieve the dreams I dreamt so long ago. You will be able to explain his face to others. Consider the story of Isit and It-is."

"It's what?"

But he had already removed his pen and started writing again. I wanted to read what he was writing, but immediately found myself standing amongst the tables again, in the same place I had started. I looked for him, but the crowd had grown larger and I could not find him.

I would have fought this if I had not been distracted by the two figures above me. I thought that the old man had said 'is it' and 'it is,' but realized then that he had spoken the names of two different people. These were the names of the man and woman who standing a short distance away from me on two different escalators that formed an X between the left and right corners of the top and bottom floors. They must have been together, for they were dressed unlike anyone else in the mall. Yet strangely enough, no one seemed to notice them. Isit was the man on the right, and It-is the lady on the other side. She had thick black hair that came down to her shoulders and he appeared to be bald—no, shaven, there was a hint of gray in his scalp. A gray so light, it was closer to white.

It-is wore a long black dress with old-fashioned white gloves that came up to her elbows. Is-it wore the opposite—white suit with black gloves. He had black tinted sunglasses while hers were reflective mirrors. Both of them had made it impossible to see their eyes.

There was no one else on the escalators. They had stepped onto them together, so that they crossed each others path at the same time, making It-is the only one visible for a brief moment. They descended through the garden and into the mass of shops, garbage cans and linoleum floors. They stepped off, turned, and continued walking at the same speed. Is-it was then on my left, and It-is on my right, until I was directly in between them, and turned so as not to lose sight. They made me feel stupid in my unappealing pants and T-shirt. I wanted to be decked out in Prada or something closer to their style.

I rushed to catch up, like a younger sibling trying to tag along. They walked side by side, without touch each other. If she hadn't been wearing a thick scarf around the middle of her body, her dress would have revealed all of her back. It was some modern, Westernized kimono, I thought, or perhaps she is hiding a scar.

They did not look hospitable at all, so I hung back a little to maintain some distance. However, they abruptly slowed down, and before I knew what was happening I was between them.

"Please" Isit said "Come with. A friend of our card player's a friend of ours."

I smiled, and even though they did not smile back, I felt welcome in their company. It-is encouraged me to say something by slightly raising her eyebrow.

"Oh, sorry" I stumbled, "My name is Phaedrus."

"Nice to meet you." She said.

"Likewise" followed Isit.

"The pleasure's mine."

We veered off the linoleum road into a dimly lit bar.

"Another act of corporate sabotage? Asked It-is, in such an ambivalent tone I wondered why she had asked it at all, or if it was some kind of rhetorical question.

"Yes" he responded, "but definitely for a good cause."

It-is and I took seats at the bar while Isit continued to stand, fixing the collar of his jacket. She handed him a cigar and he wedged it into the left side of his mouth.

"Are they there?"

She casually looked into the back of the room. In the reflective surface of her shades, a group of business men with rolled up sleeves and loosened collars were drinking beer in the back. When he turned around and faced them, everything about him changed. His posture turned gelatinous, so that he no longer gave off the powerful, enigmatic energy that seemed so impressive when I saw him on the escalator. He had become a normal man. It-is spoke into my ear as I watched him approach the table.

"First, he moves in on the target, pretending to be one of them. They take an immediate liking to him. None of them remember meeting him, but act as if they do, because he's such a great guy."

"Target?" I asked, turning around on the bar stool, attempting to see through her sunglasses. She turned away and ordered a seltzer. After squeezing its lime and sipping, she replied, "Exactly. Victim, prey, sucker, one to be assassinated. The person wanted dead by our clientele."

"You two are assassins?"

"The most merciful in the business. Most expensive too. 'Siblings of fortune' is our little joke."

"I don't understand."

Isit was drinking glasses of milk just as fast as they put drank their beers. They had all lit cigars and a dense cloud of smoke and the badly lit room made them hard to see. She took another sip, large enough to make the ice cubes clink together when she put it down.

"There was once a wealthy widow. She lived on Park Avenue. When her husband died, she became torn between wanting to move onwards and her illusory world of abandonment. Isit and I acknowledge the fact that this woman was our mother, but we never felt as though we shared her blood. One day, she came across a genie's lamp and the opportunity to make three wishes."

Because she would not loom back at me, I let my stare wander around the room. I inspected the features of her face and body, then looked down into the glass of melting ice. Occasionally the cloud of smoke in the back—which had turned totally opaque—would reveal a feature for my scrutiny. The men in the back were constantly laughing.

"But the moment she saw the genie, she had only one wish. To bare his child. She felt it was the only solution to her state of limbo. At first, the genie refused. He said it wasn't part of his contract. Eventually though, he gave up. She gave birth to us. Twins. What our mother didn't know was that the genie served a higher power, and consequentially, so did his offspring. Our father returned for us as soon as we had come of age."

She withdrew a handheld mirror and adjusted her make-up. Because her lenses were bent, I saw the reflection of the mirror, reflecting her glasses into infinity. It was a bizarre optical illusion that caused her eyes to look concave, as if I could see right through her head.

"And?"

"And so we have to work for him. And Isit is almost done, so now I go."

Everything seemed to be over for her, whereas I felt like I had been abandoned near the edge of some tall precipice. All the men in the back of the room were on the edge of their seats, about to explode with laughter, leaning into Isit as he spoke. The smoke had parted just enough to let me see the table, like the vertical lips of a lover who you dream about with such intensity that visions of her body transfer to your waking world, maintaining a gaseous consistency that only adds to the confusion of it all.

Isit then abruptly looked at his watch and walked away, leaving the men at the edge of their seats, tortuously withholding the punch-line they had expected to hear. They called to him for a considerable amount of time before giving up. He was not going back. They would have followed him, no doubt, if It-is had not replaced him as soon as he had left.

Isit had let go of his enticing ambience before approaching the men, but when It-is stood up, she magnified it. Her steps toward the table turned into the method of her self-display—lifting and resting her buttocks and chest, showing the men while at the same time showing nothing to them at all. The men immediately slid into the booth, squeezing the man in the middle of the booth.

When Isit sat down, the glass had been refilled with seltzer, only mixed this time with Absolut. Either the bartender was accustomed to this routine or Isit looked like he could use the drink. He finished half the glass.

"Now It-is delivers the punch-line."

"Excuse me?"

"That's how we do it. I tell half the joke, and she tells the punch-line. Our father tattooed it on our backs."

"You mean the genie?"

"He prefers 'triadic desire fulfillment specialist,' but yes, you could call him that. We turned sixteen and then he told me the first half and then told her the second."

"What joke?"

He spread out his arms and, in an exaggerated tone, said "The funniest joke in the world!" Then whispered to me, "she'll take that man who's sitting next to her upstairs, rent a room, and then undress in front of him, and when he reads the tattoo, he will laugh so hard his mind and body will collapse."

It-is had started to pet him affectionately, intertwining her own body with the victim's. A Sex-constructor.[22] To my surprise, Isit was no longer sitting next to me when I turned around. The old man had replaced him, and was looking at me indirectly, through his glasses, to the reflection on the table and on into my eyes. His enormous book lay on the counter, opened up to several diagrams of spirals, circles, and planets.

"I think you are here, Phaedrus, not just to observe these strange assassins, but to help all of us escape the endless cycle that each element you see here is ready to surpass. You see, existence is the means through which love learns about itself, creating opposites in a perpetual orbit around love itself. The distance of these orbits can increase when its components are understood, and yet for some strange reason, the world you see around you is stuck, and has lost the power to expand or contract. Someone is needed, Phaedrus, to allow our world to escape this perpetual state and return to the fulcrum where opposites become the same again. Once this has been done, we can expand even farther and explore existence at an even greater than the one we are in now.[23]

"Everyone you have encountered on this path of yours is stuck in the same way, and we believe that you can help us get back to the center so that we will once again be able to progress.

Go on to the next page

[22] The term "sex-constructor," is actually a technique used for coming on to women developed by three heartbreakers during the summer of 2000. As a boa–constructor wraps itself around its victim and tightens after each exhalation, one starts the sex-constructor by, for example, placing the hand on the inner thigh, and getting closer and closer each time the so called victim moves, rather than moving himself.

[23] See Illustration 6

Chapter 609

Rye Damour had not had an opportunity to couple with a woman since his wife had died. As the years went by, his job produced a multitude of conflicts every day that caused the features of his face to sink. His handsome features had become hidden, like an overgrown garden whose keeper knew what once had grown there but was all too weary of the plagues which he had brought.

Because Rye knew that he had been attractive, and that his lack of appeal was only a result of his internal conflict, he was not suspicious of the woman's enticements. It was the hope that something beautiful remained inside of him that pulled him with her to the Four Seasons hotel across the street.

Rye did not know that he had paid for the experience which waited for him in the suite. A short while ago, Rye had decided to end his life. He could no longer tolerate his life as a hypocrite.

He could not be a lawyer with morals, for such a thing did not exist. To have represented Philip Morris in court for the majority of his life—even after his wife had died of lung cancer and his daughter had begun to chain smoke—had made his life more painful than the victim's of his ultimately evil employer.

A long time ago, when he had just started working as a lawyer, he heard a rumor regarding the hidden hit men that corporations, governments, and desperate people employed to do their dirty work. One of these services apparently offered a humane death. However, Rye had not been able to extract the method used (surely humanistic murder is another oxymoron?).

This mystery was the first thought that came to his mind when he had decided to end his own life. After a considerably lengthy investigation, Rye was surprised to find that the assassin's agent was an old friend of his. A woman named Lisa, and he managed to convince her that he needed the services she offered. She refused to tell him how it would happen though, and so Rye had been waiting ever since, never knowing how he would experience the euthanasia he had paid for.

The woman he had left the bar with did not want to hear about the conversation he had been having prior to their departure. She preferred the comfort of his lips. The subtle exploration of his body with her gloved hands. He wanted to tell her about the joke that man had told him, and how he wished he had heard the punch-line. He wanted to tell her what a masterful storyteller he had been, and how even though he did not remember meeting him, he felt as though he knew him. But she would not let him talk, and supplicated her request of silence by silently communicating with her body.

On any other night, he would have acted with the anxiousness of dreamers who have waited too long to be gratified. But his extraordinary recollections of the night's events had caused him to embrace the mystery of prolonged hope with the aqueous fluidity that lover's use to savor something good.

He found himself undressed in the large, buoyant bed, kneeling behind the enigma who had aroused the sense of hope and mystery that every married man must miss.

'*Everything is finally making sense*' he thought as he moved into position, placing his hands over her thighs and beginning the process of physical love. He thought he had forgotten how to join a rhythm, but his instinctual sense took over. He had not forgotten anything.

And just before he finished, she pulled away the silk that had been covering her back, revealing the tattoo upon her skin. He read the sentence instantly, but only recognized it as the punch line of the strange man's joke at the moment of his climax with the woman. And the humor of it all—of the joke and the complexities within his life and the irony contained by both—caused him to laugh as he came with the manifold forces of pleasure and happiness and that which stays unknown forever, until his total self could not accommodate the truth. In this way, he left the world. Without surprise or hesitancy.

It-is sank into the bed, alone. She wondered the same thoughts that she always wondered when her victims vanished. If they had died or simply rearranged their matter to an invisible state of understanding. If what she did was ethical. If Jesus had laughed.

As usual, she spent the night in the same bed that her victim had died in. She rolled her body around in the sheets—the last two things her victims ever felt.

Misconception:

From A to B

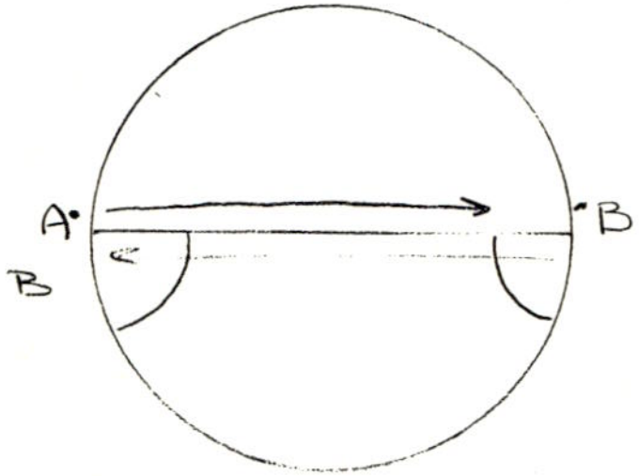

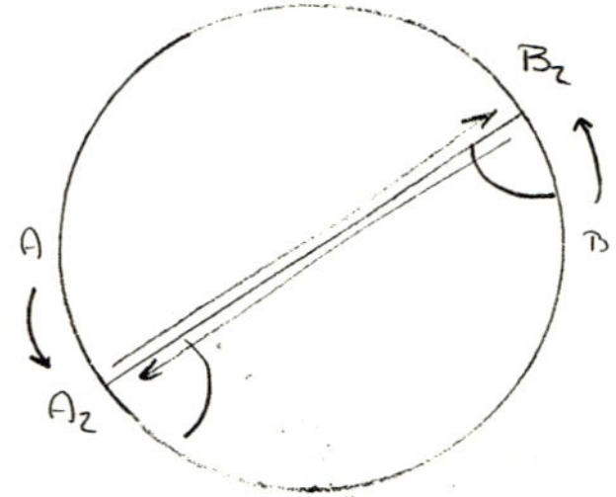

If destination moves, starting point has to move in order to stay balanced

In Reality

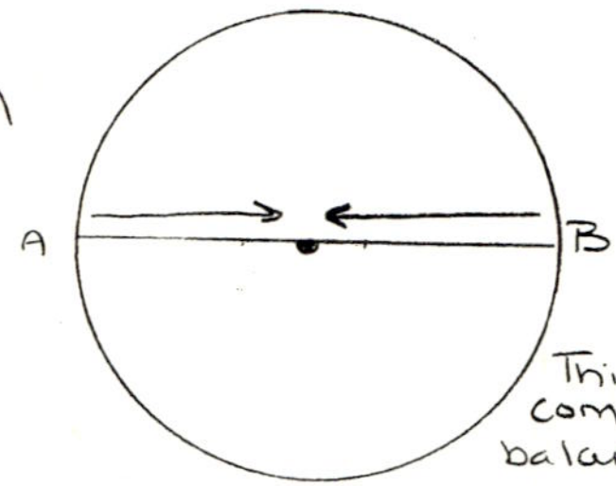

Like seesaw, destination and starting point approach each other, equidistant from center.

This can be compared to balancing a simple algebraic equation

once both points meet, it is possible to reach any destination desired, because there is nothing to balance. Everything is in the center:

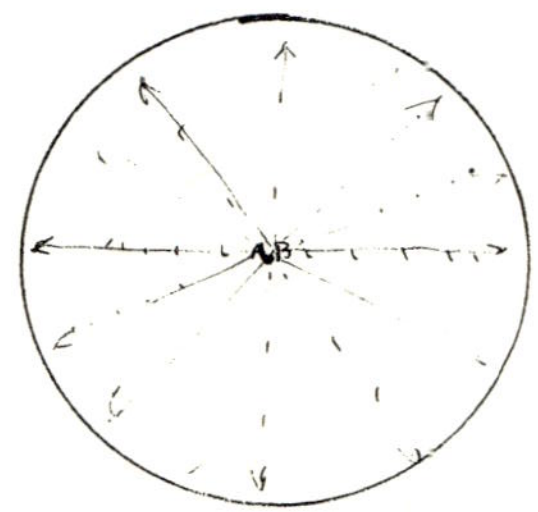

A→ ←B $\pi^{\frac{9xy}{3}} = \pi^{3xy}$

A→ ←B $\frac{9xy}{3} = 3xy$

A⟶ ←B $4(9x/3)$ $4(3x)$

A⟶ ⟵B $9x/3 = 3x$

A⟶ —B $x = x$

ILLUSTRATION ② A

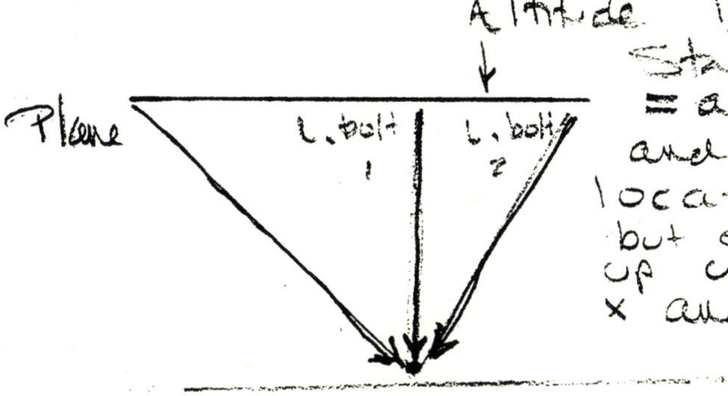

Plane + lightning starts at = altitudes (y) and diff locations (x) but ends up with same x and y

Plane = P

Light. Bolt 1, 2 = L1, L2

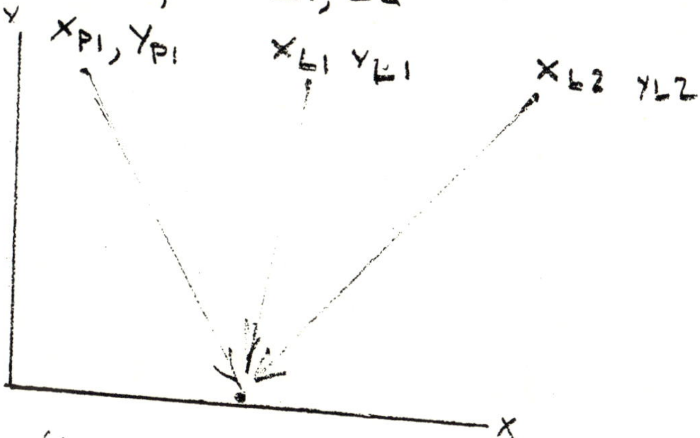

$y_{P1} = y_{L1} = y_{L2}$

$x_{P1} \neq x_{L1} \neq x_{L2}$

— start

$y_{P1} = y_{L1} = y_{L2}$

$x_{P1} = x_{L1} = y_{L2}$

— end

Like pyramid →

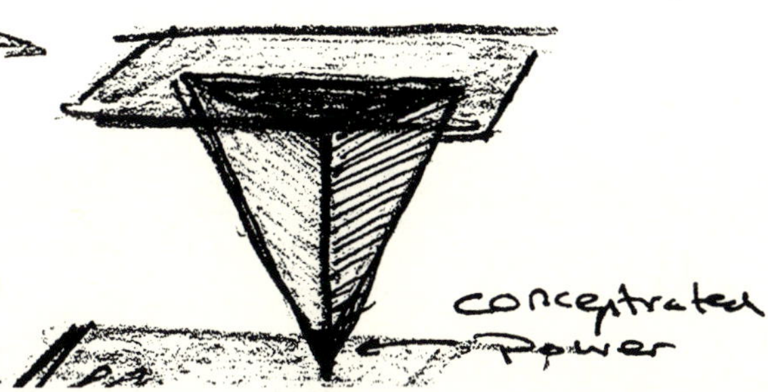

ILLUSTRATION #3

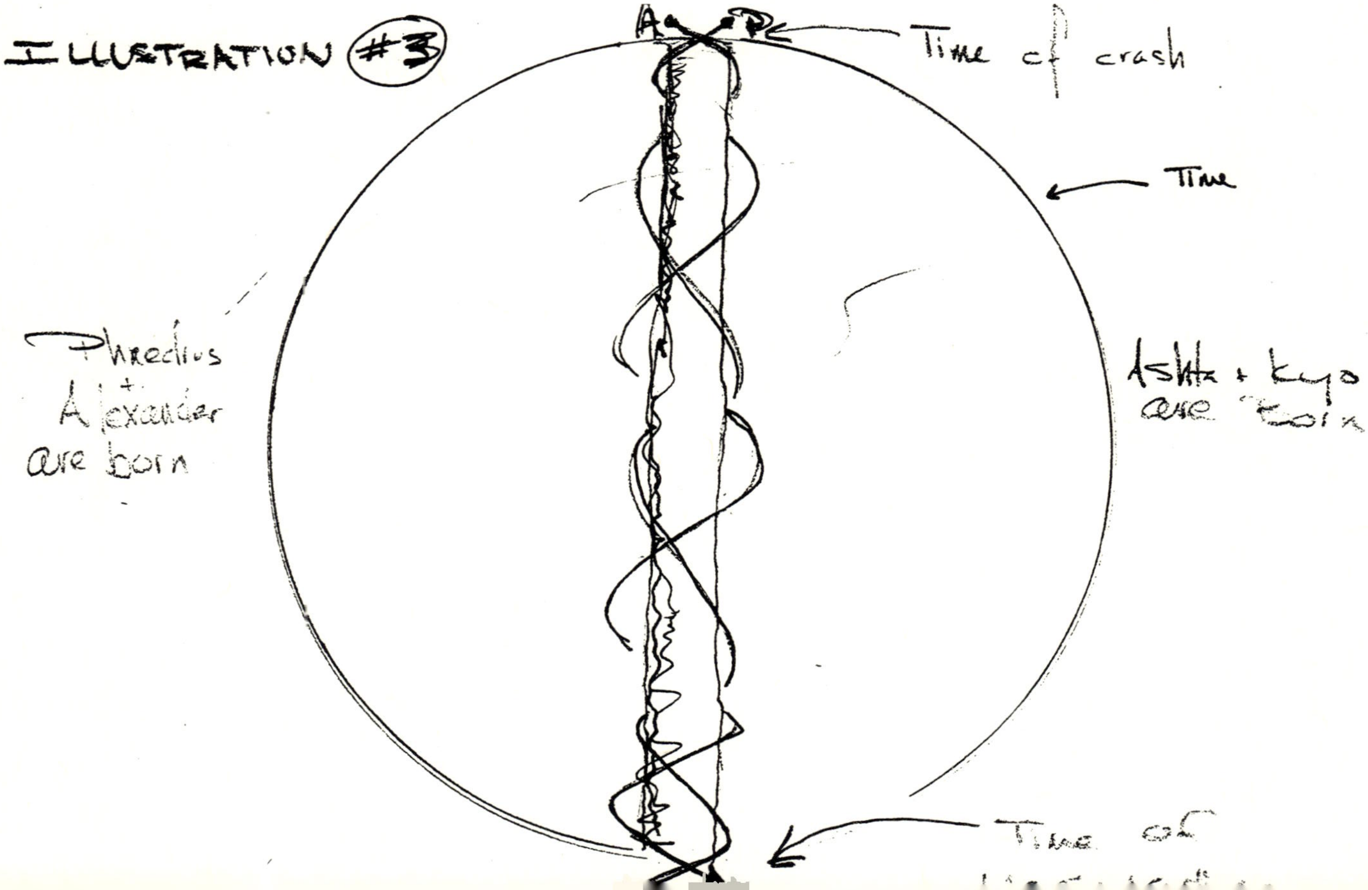

ILLUS (4)

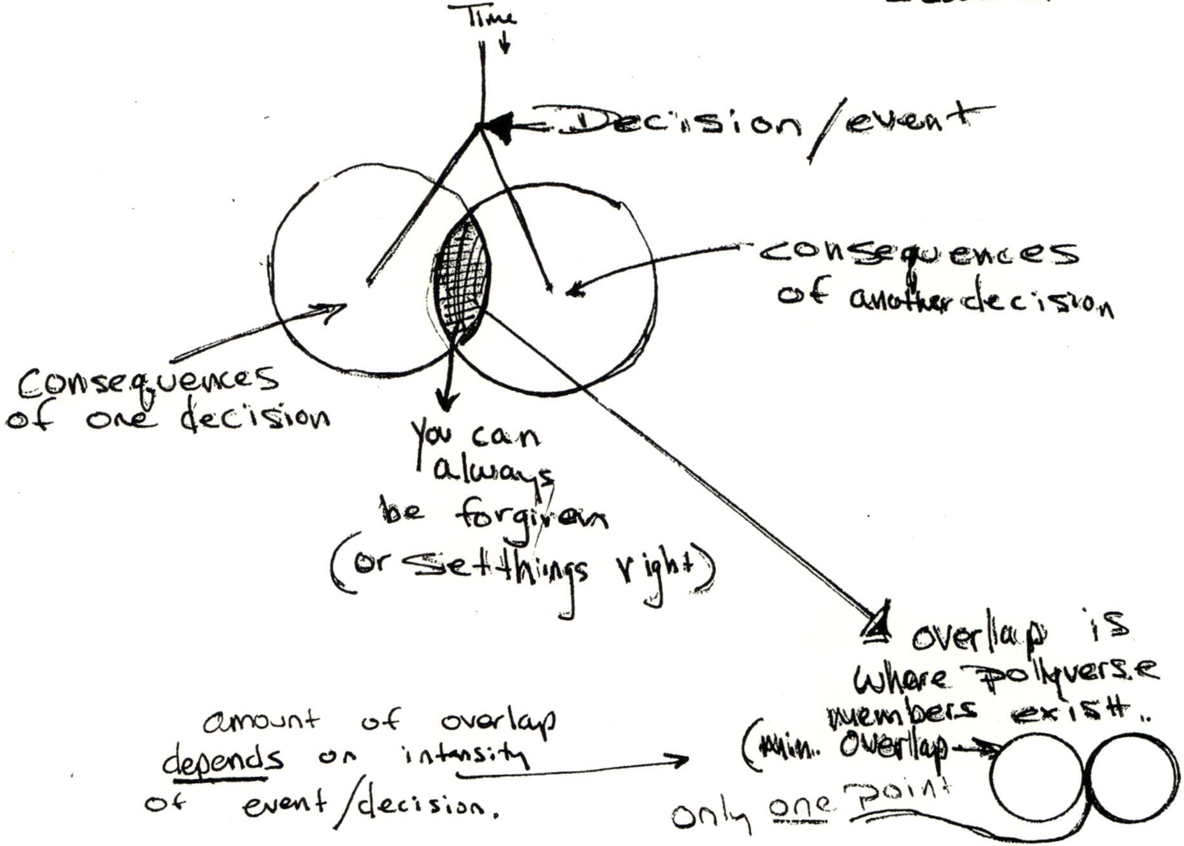
Time
Decision/event
consequences
of another decision
Consequences
of one decision
You can
always
be forgiven
(or set things right)
overlap is
where polyverse
members exist..
(min. overlap
only one point
amount of overlap
depends on intensity
of event/decision.

ILLUS 5A

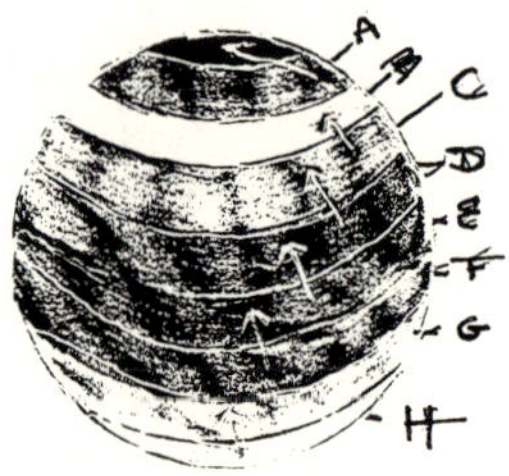

View	Horizon
A	(??)
B	A
C	B
D	C
E	D
F	E
G	F
H	G

|Horizon| = A+B+C+D+E+F+G.

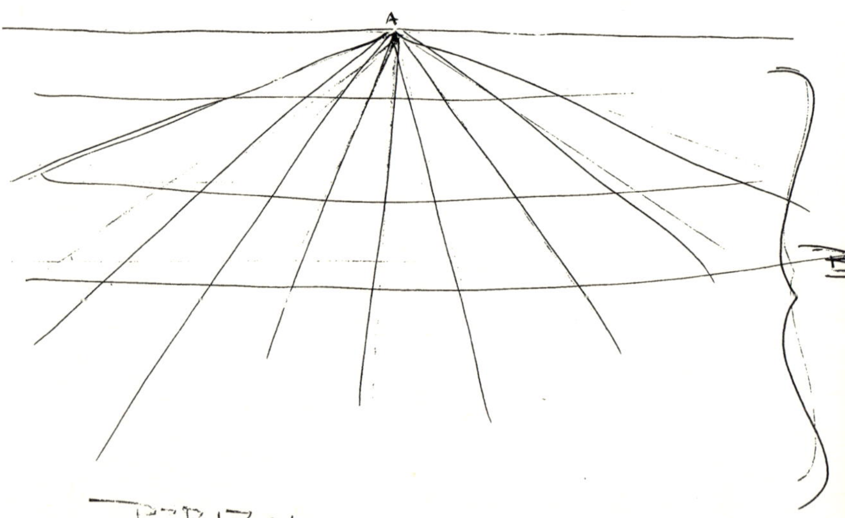

PERIZON

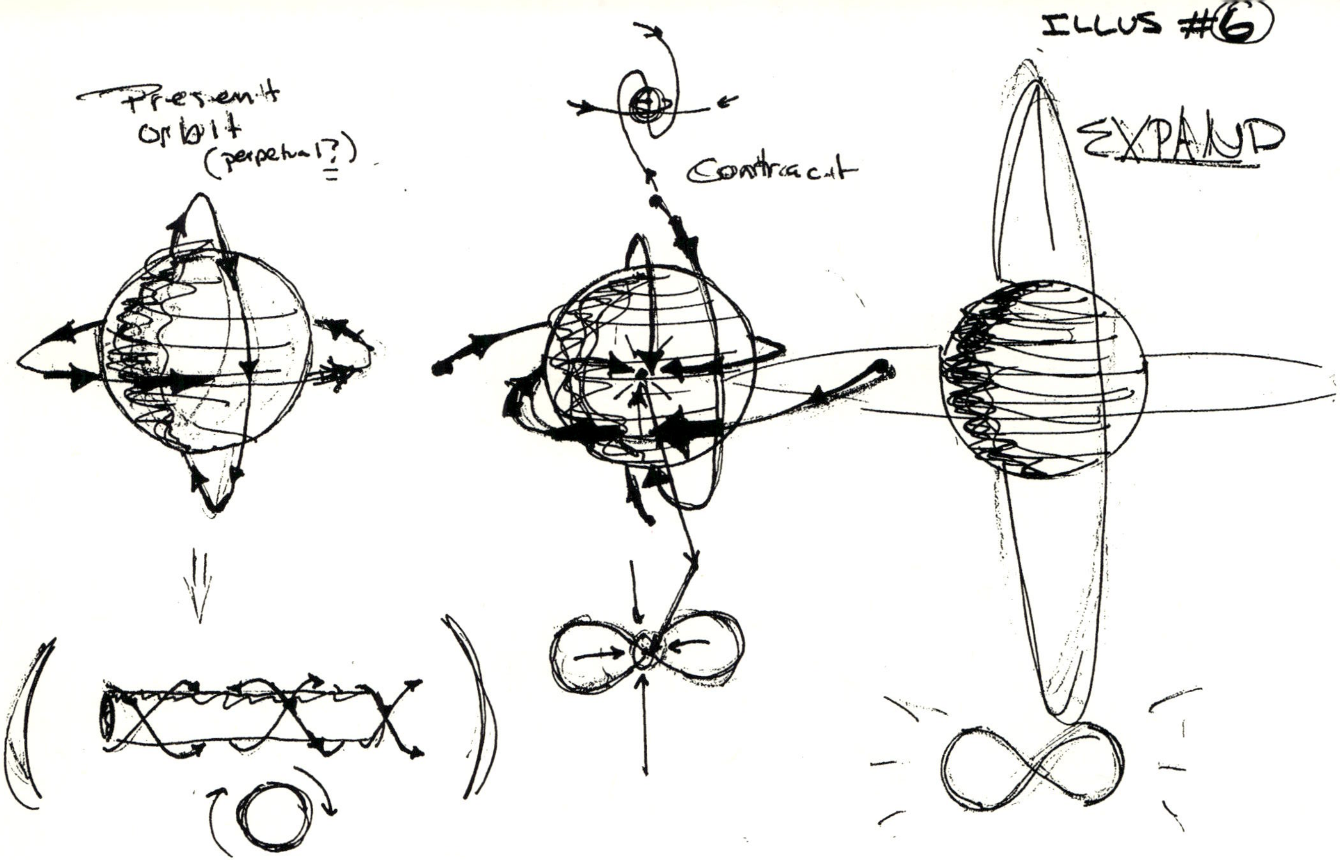
ILLUS #6
Present
orbit
(perpetual?)
Contracat
EXPAND

ILLUS. 7

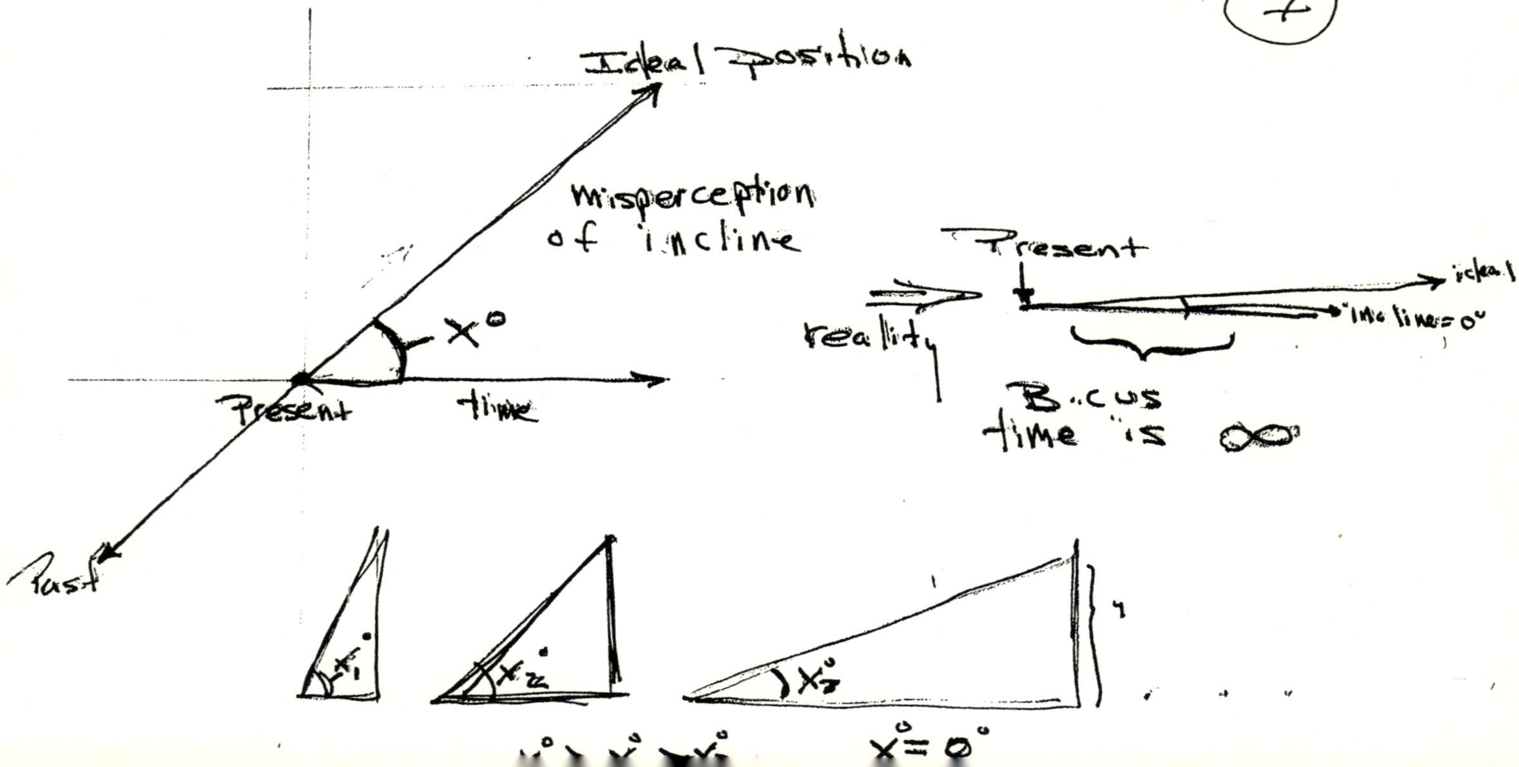
Ideal position
misperception of incline
x°
Present
time
Past
Present
ideal
incline = 0°
reality
time is ∞
x_1°
x_2°
x_3°
$x^\circ = 0^\circ$

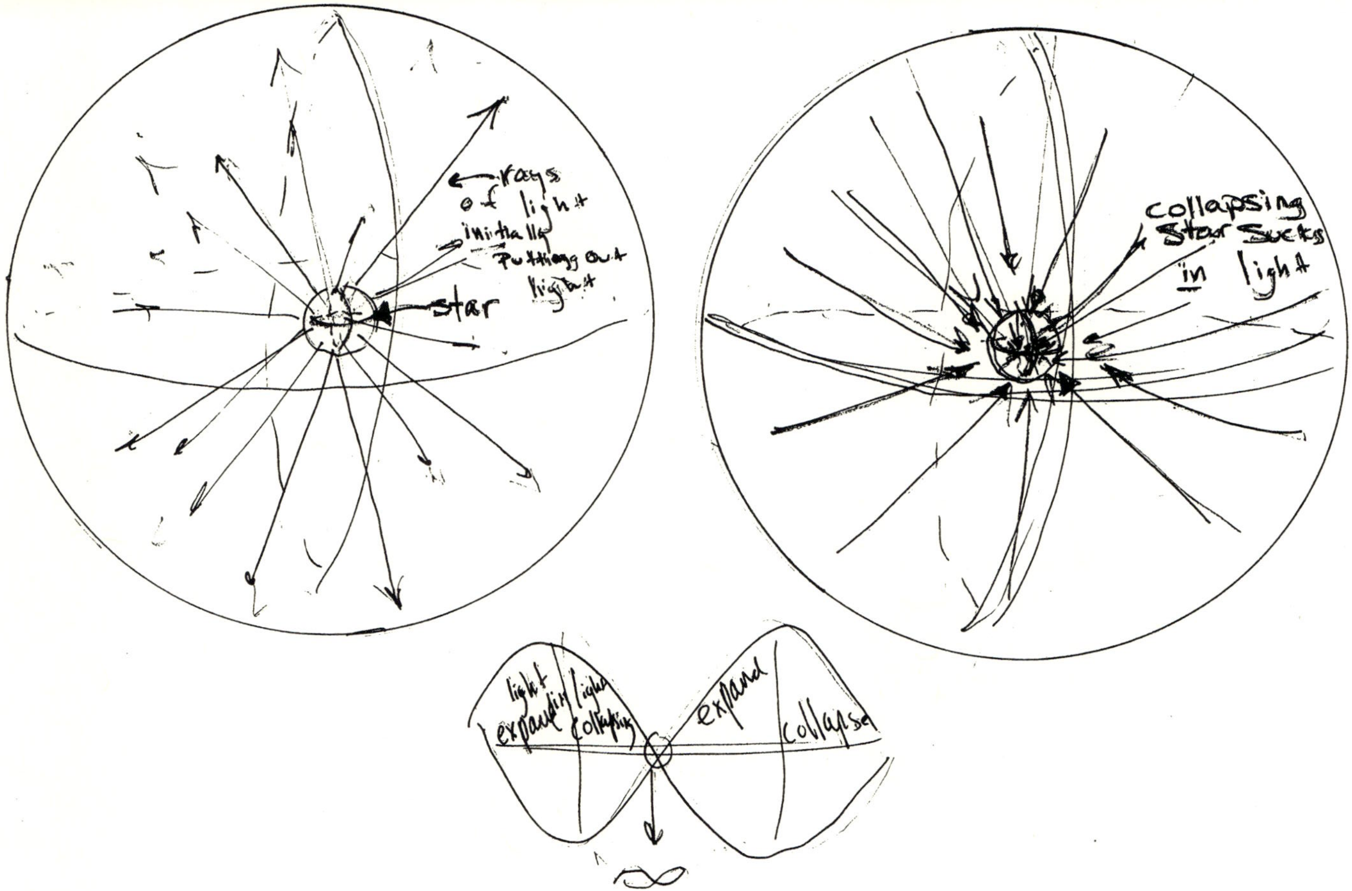
rays of light initially putting out light
star
collapsing star sucks in light
light expanding
light collapsing
expand
collapse
∞

Notes on comparing ∞ with waves, further investigation of cyclic existence

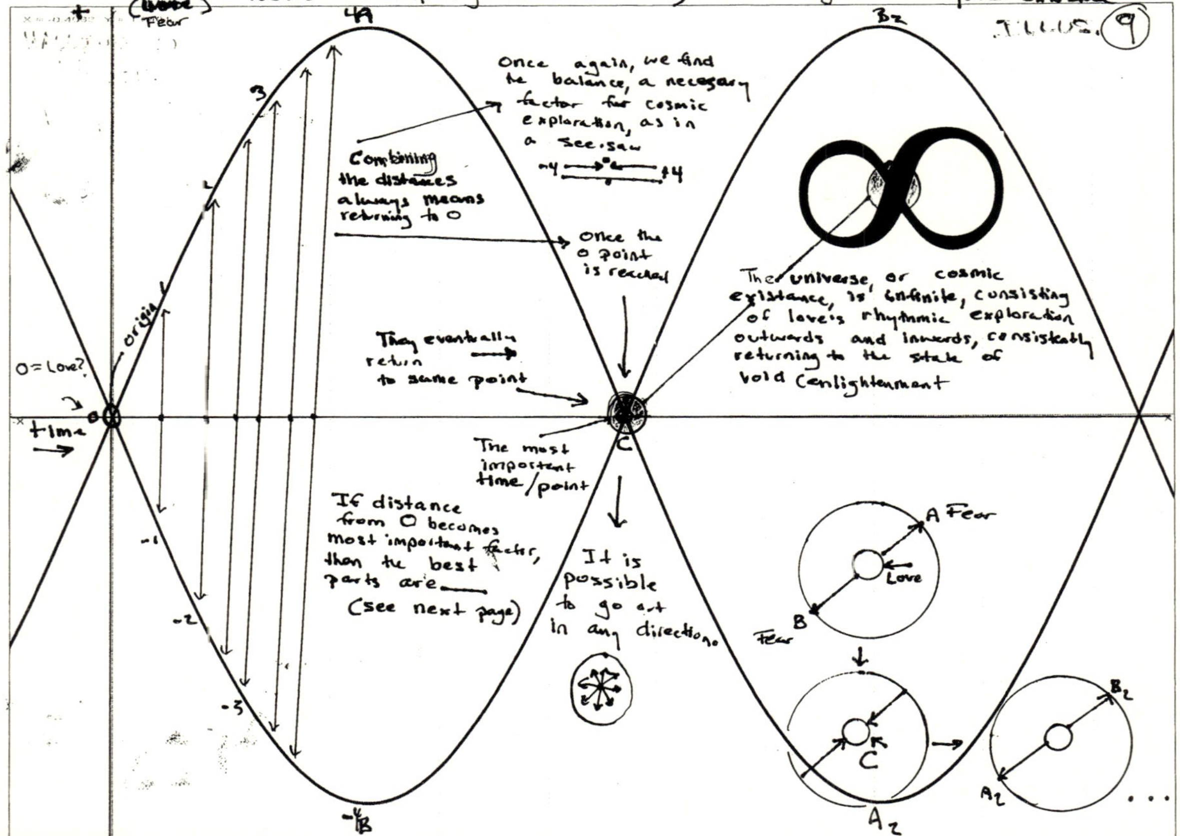

9A

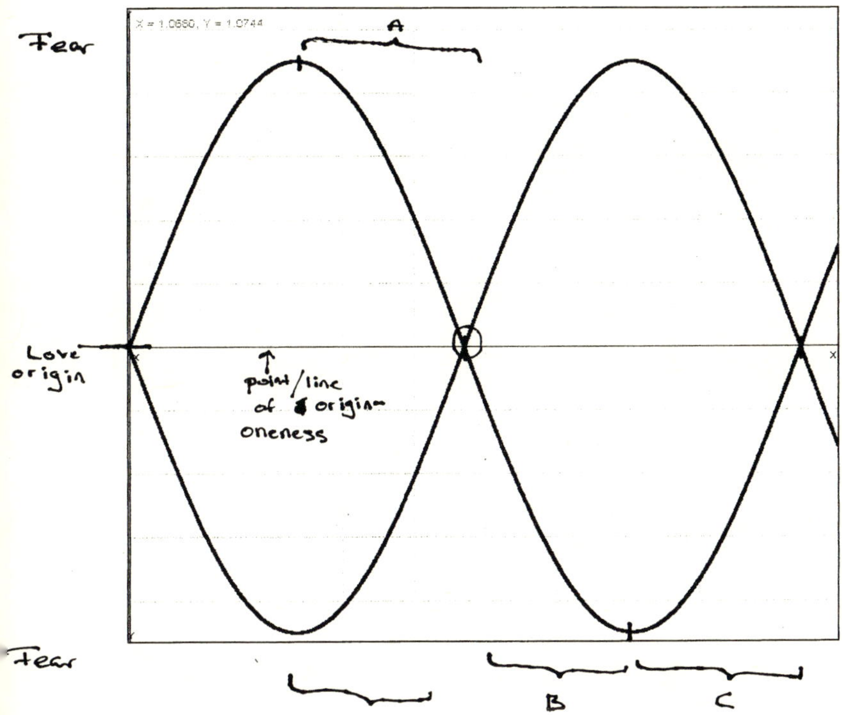

Points A and C, and section in between, are most desirable for Red, as well as green.

This is diff from graph of depression, or emotional state, where distance from O is desired in + direction, and avoided in − direction

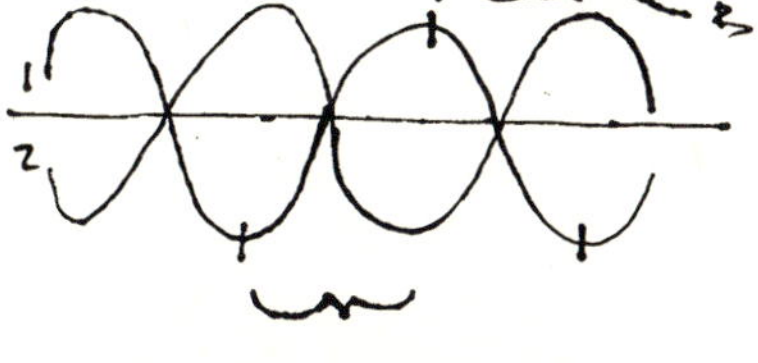

A becomes good for 1, but opposite for 2, and vice versa for Section B.

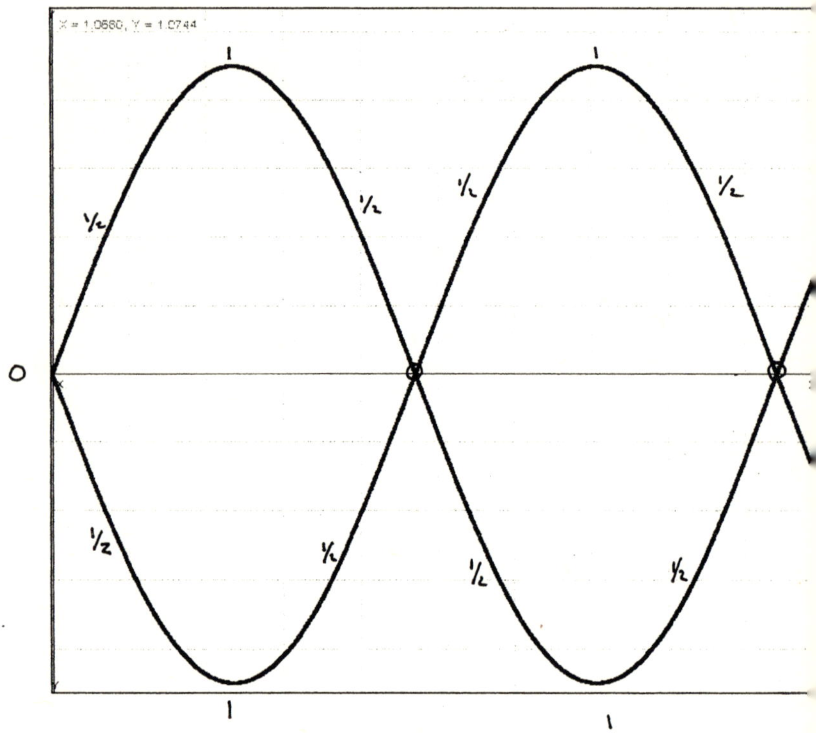

If the O point is subject to such study, it must be necessary to also consider the more frequent positions. There are 3 O points in a normal cycle, 4 1 points, and 8 mid points

If a seeker of the ultimate goal is to reach his destination — that is recognize and utilize the O position — surely he/she must know what to do in the more common points

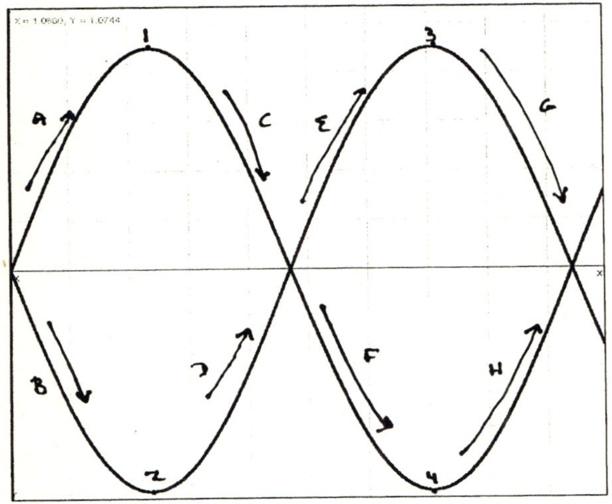

Mid points, being the most common positions from love, ~~can~~ play the role of ~~t~~ most comfortable, recognized point.

It is a point of no return, due to its ability to become a rhythm on its own, while undisturbing the macrocosmic rhythm. Ultimately, every aspect of existence is a microcosmic rhythm of the universal beat, so understanding the mid point helps one understand his relationship to not only fear and love, but to other manifestations of the cycle.

The mid points make up the main machinery of the cycle, connecting the maximums with 0 points

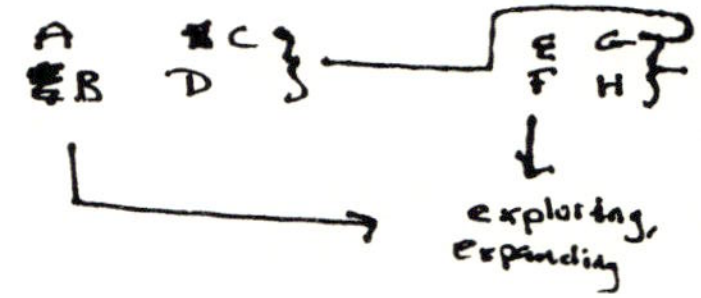

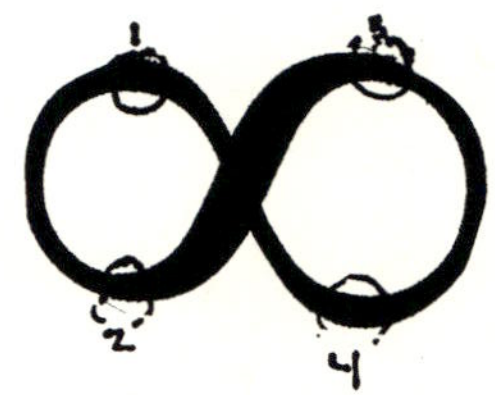

The maximums are usually responded to in different ways (Although they are the same distances from love, they are opposite directions, meaning opposite experiences.)

Reaching 1/2 the max point* ~~often~~ can result in confusion, which, if not cautious, can confuse the spirit into fearing the return. →

meaning 1+3 illustrate 1/2 of the kinds of *

9D

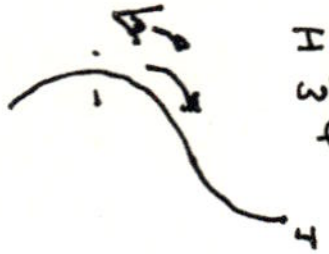

It is like gravity, which creates desire for superiority or conformity

→ compare with point at which an arcing object momentarily loses sensation of gravity.

1,3 contains a point where there is a decrease in kinetic energy, or at least a window where potential energy can be considered.

The perpetual, kinetic movement of the cycle can be confusing to a reality where both kinetic and potential energy are used in greater varieties (more 'Potential')

9D

2 + 4

The other max points are more straightforward – the gut-wrenching momentum does not cause confusion, only direct discomfort, for it is the most 'down' position. However, once passing the positions, the 0 point is in view.

HALLOWEEN

9E

Simplest Form:

- single Point
  Only place of reference
  Love is complete and in
  most pure form, but has
  no way to compare itself.
  It has nothing to compare with
  So it doesn't know what it is

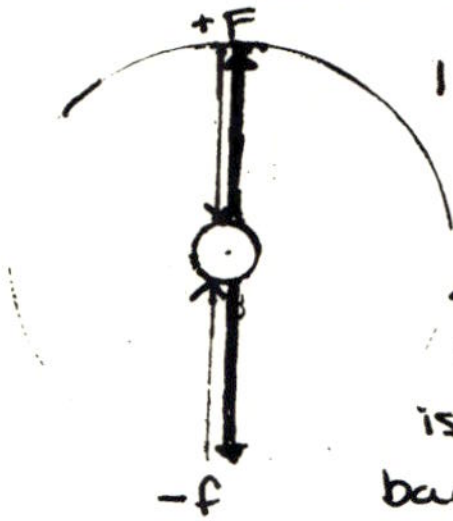

1 D ← straight line in space, if infinite, bends (e=mc²)

Love illuminates things outside at various distances so

← Distance 1 a circle it is

it illuminates what it isn't — fears, then retracts back.

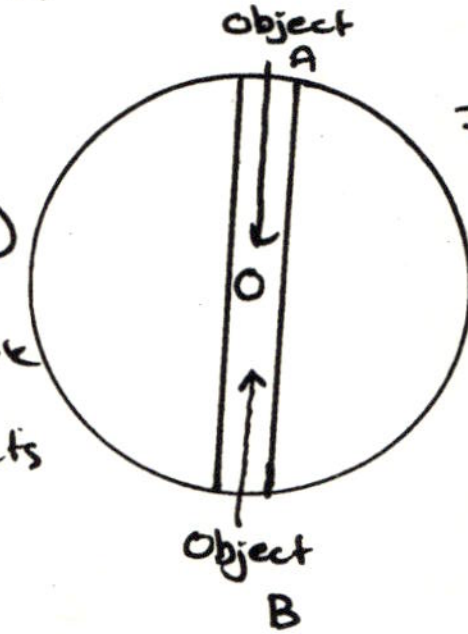

It is comparable to a couple of objects released from opposite sides of a planet, through the center, at the same time

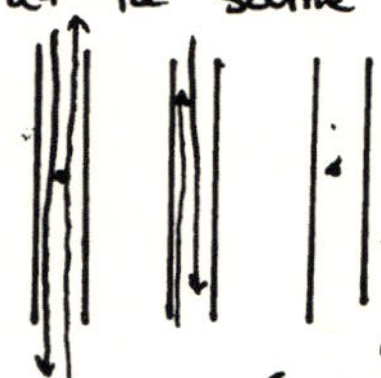

objects continually move to center than away a distance that is just a little less (or not, if experience is considered perpetual)

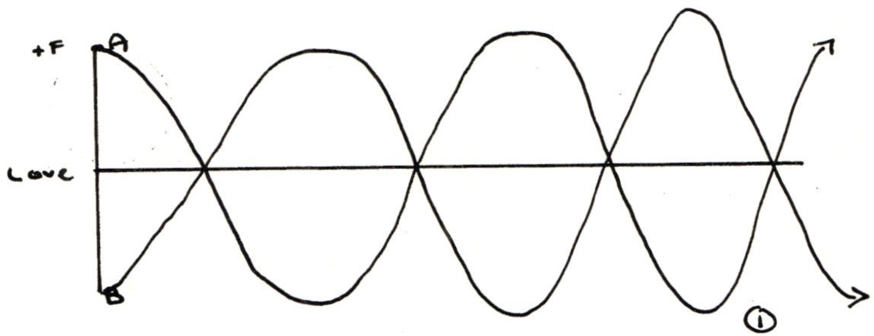

← perpetual finite

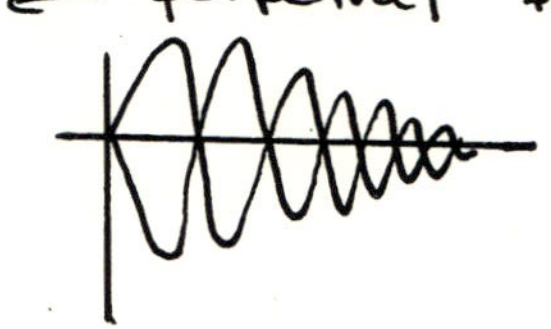

HALLOWEEN

9F

2D

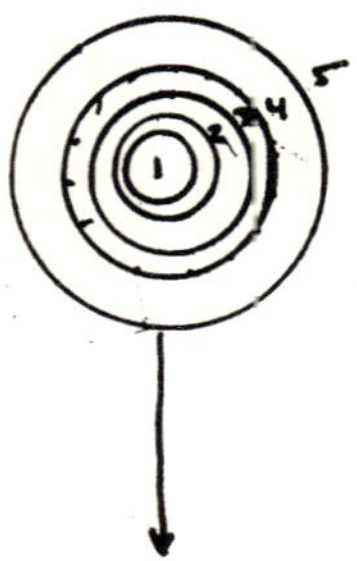

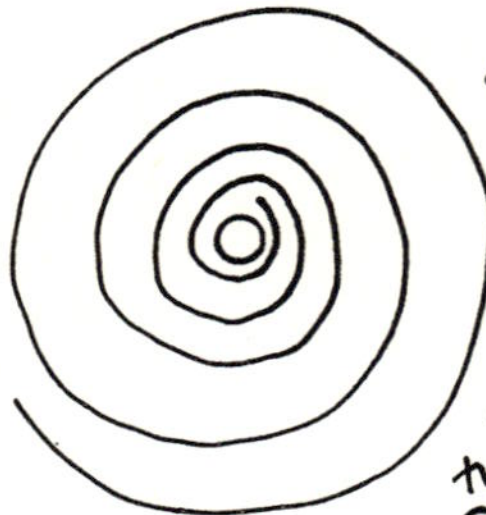

With Two Dimensions, Love can expand at constant rate, comparing itself with more and more, meaning the farther away, the more you find

Closer to love means ~~more~~ better ability to communicate/know/control/compare because you are a part of it.

9F

3D

The cons[illegible] of states were fears strays at constant rate from love, allowing the two to co-exist. With perpetual co-existence, there can be manifestations of things consisting of both → co-existence,

Consider:

Love expands in all directions

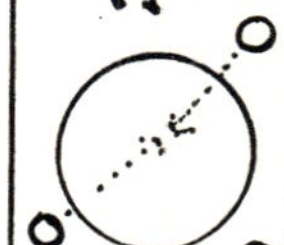

two masses of fear equal in every way except on different sides of love retract towards it, but due to each other, ~~[illegible]~~ bend slightly.

They end up orbiting love, perpetually experience the different fears at one specific distance at opposite times

More on 3L

The relationship between love and the two fears can be illustrated as a double helix

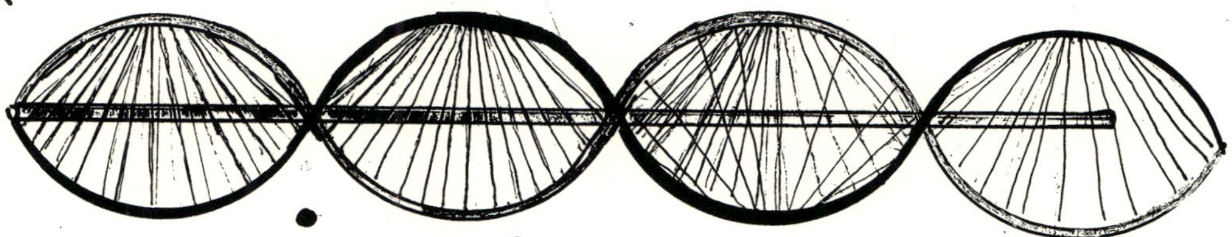

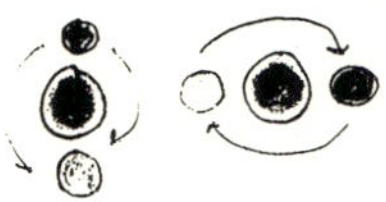

Distance from either fear to love or other fear is always the same and always equal to the other, with Love in middle